the SWEETEST GAME

J. STERLING

OTHER BOOKS IN THIS SERIES
The Perfect Game: Book One
The Game Changer: Book Two
The Sweetest Game: Book Three

OTHER BOOKS BY J. STERLING
Chance Encounters
In Dreams

Table of Contents

The Wedding · 1

Married Life · 6

Breaking Bones · 17

I'm A Baseball Player · 37

Being Hurt Doesn't Work For Us · 45

Welcome to the Big Apple · 59

New York State of Mind · 68

It's Just Sex · 86

Slow Recovery · 102

Traded · 117

Slightly Emotional · 134

Moving Home · 163

Happy Birthday · 189

Hard to Have a Family on the Road · 219

You Miss Out · 226

The End of a Dream · 237

Our New Lives · 251

Epilogue · 263

About the Author · 273

Dedication

This book is for everyone who found their
dreams in the stars ...

And for each person who helped push them
by the feet so they could reach.

Note from the Author

This book is part of a series. If you haven't read the previous books, it is highly recommended that you do so. *The Perfect Game* is the first book, followed by *The Game Changer*. Both books are available in paperback from various retailers. They are also available in E-Book format.

The Wedding

Cassie

Hands on my hips, I looked my best friend in the eye and shook my head as she turned to reapply her lipstick in the mirror.

"Don't look at me like that," Melissa snapped as she forced back a grin.

"Oh, I'll look at you like that, all right. I'll look at you like that all night if I want. Are you trying to kill my future brother-in-law?" I teased, knowing that less than two minutes ago she was locked in Dean's room doing who-knows-what while I sat in Jack's room waiting for her.

She narrowed her eyes before turning to face me. "Maybe."

Frustrated, I rolled my eyes. "Try not to. I've grown attached."

After applying a new coat of lipstick, she smacked her lips together before moving next to me. "You look gorgeous, by the way." Her hands touched the back of my hair as she rearranged specific strands while I smoothed the nonexistent wrinkles from my knee-length white dress.

"Thanks. So do you." Despite being annoyed with my pint-sized pal, I couldn't help but smile.

"So, was your dad pissed about not walking you down the aisle?"

I sucked in a breath. The last thing I wanted on my wedding day was to feel bad about any of my decisions. The choice of walking alone or with my father weighed heavily on me at first. But I eventually decided that having my father walk me toward my life with Jack and then handing me over to him would all be for show. And I knew in that moment that I didn't want anyone to be responsible for "giving me away," least of all the one man in my life who had disappointed me more than any other.

It only seemed right that I walk down the aisle on my own and join Jack freely to start our lives together, since it was my choice, my decision, my heart waiting for me at the end of that aisle. After all, no one could give me to the one person I'd already given myself to years ago.

"He was definitely hurt at first. But I don't think he truly got the message I was trying to convey. I think he just wanted to walk me down the aisle because that's what a dad is supposed to do."

"Oh well. Maybe he should have been a better dad," Melissa said in a sharp tone.

I shrugged. "Hopefully after he sees how untraditional everything is today, he'll understand and be less disappointed."

Music filtered through the open windows and into the living room where Melissa and I stood waiting. I took in a deep breath and bit my bottom lip as excitement surged through me.

"Oh my gosh! It's time!" Melissa moved toward the glass patio door and let out a little gasp as she peeked outside. "Ooh, it's so pretty, Cass!" She gave me a hug and whispered, "I'll see you out there," then stepped out and slowly made her way down the makeshift aisle.

After taking a deep breath, I followed her lead, pausing briefly at the doorway. She was right. Gran and Gramps' backyard had been transformed into a place of wonder. Candles cast tiny shadows everywhere as the sun began to sink behind the trees. A myriad of tiny lights twinkled in the tree branches.

When I stepped outside, my gaze landed on the mason jars filled with quarters and candles that lined the aisle, and I couldn't help but smile as my heart filled with the sheer amount of love I felt for Jack. Still smiling, I looked down the aisle and immediately locked on to his chocolate-brown eyes. The air whisked from my lungs for a moment at the sight of him standing there in his charcoal-gray suit, waiting for me with a shit-eating grin plastered on his face.

I had to stop myself from running to him and leaping into his arms. Although I don't think he would have minded.

Once at the altar, Jack reached out and took my hand in his, caressing it with his thumb in a sensual gesture that sent tingles throughout my body. "You look beautiful," he whispered as he leaned toward me.

"And you look hot," I whispered back, then gave him a wink.

Gramps cleared his throat and both Jack and I stifled a laugh. Jack's grandfather looked serious as he welcomed our friends and family to this "special day," before diving right into the ceremony.

Looking into Jack's eyes, I swear I only heard a few things that Gramps said. My mind spun as I thought back to the journey Jack and I had traveled, from the pits of hell we'd been through to where we were now. We had come so far together.

I glanced briefly at Jack's brother, Dean, who stood next to him, but his eyes were fixed on the petite brunette standing next to me. Shaking my head softly, I smiled before returning my gaze to the man who held my heart.

When it came time to exchange vows, mine a little more tearful than Jack's. My heart melted at the sight of him getting choked up, and when he cleared his throat to regain his composure, I lost all of mine.

"I love you," I confessed through my joyful tears.

Jack reached for my face, wiping away my tears with his thumbs as he tilted his head and leaned his face toward me for a kiss.

"Uh-uh! Wait!" Gramps called out, interrupting the moment as Jack froze, my cheeks still held between his hands. Gramps paused a beat, then his face split into a wide grin as he announced proudly, "I now pronounce you man and wife. Jack?"

"Yes, Gramps?" Jack's voice rose in pitch as he remained frozen in place, and the crowd laughed.

"You may kiss your beautiful bride," Gramps pronounced before slamming his bible shut.

"It's about time," Jack said before crushing his lips against mine. Cheers and enthusiastic shouts filled my ears at first, but they quickly faded away in that moment. Soon, all I heard was the sound of my heart rapidly beating in my ears. And all I could feel was Jack's hands on my skin, and his tongue gently tasting mine.

Already on shaky legs, I grabbed Jack's shoulders for balance as he slowly pulled away, breaking our first kiss as husband and wife.

"Ladies and gentlemen, I'd like to present for the very first time, Mr. and Mrs. Carter." Gramps smiled wide.

"Baby-making time," Jack whispered in my ear before grabbing my hand and pulling us from the altar.

Heat spread across my cheeks as I choked back a response, but followed him anyway. I'd follow that man anywhere.

Married Life

Jack

Bright morning light filtered in through the curtains as I opened my eyes to the sound of Gran and Gramps placing dishes and silverware on the kitchen table. My room was closest to the kitchen, so whenever they banged around in there, it always woke me up. For a second, I was reminded of my high school days, when the smell of Gran's fresh-cooked waffles would waft down the hallway before school. With a smile, I remembered what day it was and focused my attention on the blonde hair splayed across my arm.

My wife, Cassie, lay curled up next to me, her ass pressed tightly up against my groin.

My wife.

Someone actually loved me enough to not only put up with my shit, but to agree to put up with it for the rest of her life. She was probably insane on some level, but I'd take it. Whatever kept this woman by my side was fine by me. I wasn't sure what it was about being married, but the pieces that used to spin out of control inside me actually felt settled now. Knowing that Cassie had vowed to be mine forever filled me with a sense of comfort I'd never known I was missing.

In that moment, I felt like I could do anything. I could put on a cape, sprout some wings, and save the whole fucking world if I wanted to. And the best part was, the girl by my side wasn't going anywhere. She'd sew a *J* on that cape and watch me fly if I asked her to.

How did I just revert to a twelve-year-old with superhero fantasies? Fucking loser.

I reached my arm around Cassie's bare waist, my fingers exploring the side of her body I couldn't see. She moaned and my dick throbbed to life.

"Good morning, wife," I whispered against her face, before kissing the lobe of her ear and sucking it into my mouth.

Cassie moaned again before turning to face me, her gorgeous green eyes beaming. "Good morning, husband."

Husband.

Fuck yeah, I'm your husband. I think that means I'm legally allowed to kill anyone who fucks with her, right? Right.

Leaning down, I pulled her lower lip between my teeth and nibbled playfully. Without warning, I pushed my tongue into her open mouth, moving it in sync with hers. I fucking ached to be inside her. Literally. Fucking. Ached.

"I need you," I breathed out between kisses.

Her hands reached for my lower back, her fingers pulling at my skin to move me into position on top of her. I did as she silently asked, and she pushed her knees apart in welcome. "I guess that's a yes?" I joked, sliding inside her before she changed her mind.

"Oh God, Jack," she moaned, then bit her lip. "Go slow."

"Jesus, Cassie. Do you know how hard it is to go slow when you feel this fucking good?" I attempted to manage my thrusts, but my dick was uncooperative. Like it had a mind of its own, it betrayed the commands from my brain. "I'm sorry, babe, but it won't listen."

She giggled underneath me as a line formed between her eyebrows. "What won't listen?"

"My dick," I breathed out.

Her hips moved beneath me, rising and falling in perfect time against me, with me, whatever. "I'm not going to last," I warned, trying my best to slow the inevitable.

Those beautiful green eyes met mine before she gripped the back of my neck and pulled my mouth to hers. Our tongues explored each other with increasingly frantic desperation. I moved in and out of her perfection, my hard-on growing with each thrust.

"I feel you getting bigger inside me." Her breath was hot against my mouth. "It's such a turn-on, Jack."

"You really shouldn't have said that." Those words were all it took to send me over the edge. With one last thrust, I lost myself inside of her. Cassie's mouth fell open as pleasure coursed through her body. I watched as she found her own release and shuddered when it was done.

"God, you're beautiful. I love you so much," I said as I ran my fingers through her hair.

She smiled and said, "I love you too. Always," and I was instantly reminded of how lucky I was to have her.

"Always," I agreed. "We should get up. I smell Gran's cooking and they're already in the kitchen."

Face flushed, she buried her head into my pillow. "Do you think they heard us?"

I laughed. "They didn't hear us. But we're married now, so we can do this stuff."

"Jack! Don't be disrespectful."

"Me? You're the disrespectful one," I teased before planting a kiss on her forehead. "Now get up. Unless you plan on eating breakfast naked. Honestly, I don't think Gramps would mind. Or Dean."

Her face twisted in mock horror and she smacked me playfully. "You're disgusting."

A little while later, we settled into our seats at the table and I noticed Dean heading our way. I palmed a blueberry muffin and waited. He walked through the entryway and I hurled the muffin.

"Seriously?" He looked down to see the crumbled pastry at his feet.

"Jack! Don't throw food!" Gran scolded and I shrugged.

"Nothing says good morning like a muffin to your gut," I teased and Cassie swatted me in the arm.

Dean's eyes narrowed. "Hit him harder next time, Sis. Like this." He walked over to me and socked me square in the right shoulder.

The chair screeched as I scooted out of it and chased after my little brother. He ducked and weaved throughout the kitchen,

Gran yelling in the background and Gramps laughing at our antics, before I finally caught him and started whaling on his shoulders.

"Stop hitting me, you dick!" Dean yelled as he attempted to pull his shirt from my grasp.

"Don't hit me in front of my wife." I released the death grip I had on his clothes and watched as he stood up straight, brushing off his bicep where I'd just hit him.

"You just wanted an excuse to say that."

"Say what?" I mocked with fake confusion.

"Wife." Dean looked over at Cassie for support, who watched us with a grin on her face and shook her head, refusing to get involved.

"Stop acting like you're twelve again and eat some breakfast," Gran insisted.

"Yeah, Jack. Stop acting like you're twelve." Dean shoved me before running to his seat and slamming his ass down.

"You two are ridiculous," Cassie remarked. "This smells amazing, Gran. Thank you so much."

"You're welcome. I'm just so happy to have you all here," Gran said with a smile before placing full plates of food at the center of the table.

Dean lifted a waffle with his fork and I swatted at it with mine, causing it to fall on the table. "You're such a jackass," my brother whined.

"Dean! Language." The scolding from Gran had become all too familiar whenever we were together.

"He was being a jackass, hon," Gramps noted and I stifled a

laugh.

A voice called out from the front door, and I noticed Dean stop midbite when he realized it was Melissa. "Knock-knock! Anyone home?"

"Yay! Melis!" Cassie jumped up from her seat and ran out of the kitchen as Dean glared across the table at me.

"You could have warned me she was coming over."

I shrugged and shoved a bite of waffle in my mouth, mumbling around it, "Didn't know."

"Liar."

"It's not my fault you two can't get your shit together, so don't get all PMS'y on me like a little bitch."

"Jack!" Gran said sharply. "Apologize to your brother right now."

Gramps pinned me with a disapproving look over his glasses. "That *was* uncalled for."

I chewed my food extra slowly, my gaze never leaving Dean's. "Sorry," I mumbled before narrowing my eyes and adding, "that you can't make the girl fall in love with you."

Dean shook his head and looked away as he finished the bite in his mouth with a scowl.

My beautiful wife walked back into the kitchen with her fun-sized best friend, Melissa, following close behind.

"Hi, everyone," Melissa said cheerfully.

Gran gave her a big smile. "Good morning, dear. Are you hungry? Let me grab you a plate." She started to stand but Cassie stopped her.

"I'll do that. You eat."

Melissa pushed Cassie toward her chair and shook her head.

"I already ate, but thank you."

"So, Fun-Size, did you have a good time yesterday?" I asked suggestively, trying to get her to admit she actually liked my brother as more than a friend. Dean froze and tipped his head to the side, obviously waiting to hear her answer.

She stared straight at him as she spoke without blinking, "It was the most fun I've had in a long time. How about you?"

I laughed. "Considering I married the girl of my dreams, I'll say I had more than just fun yesterday."

Melissa slid into an open chair at the table and asked, "So, when are you guys leaving?"

"Our flight leaves tonight at nine," Cassie answered, her voice deflated.

"Why can't y'all just stay forever? Screw New York!" Melissa shouted in an overly animated voice, and I noticed Dean rubbing his temples.

"What's the matter, Dean?" she asked with a laugh. "Head hurt?" She tilted her head as she goaded him playfully.

He glared at her and gave her a sharp nod before turning to me. "You can't stay any longer, can you?"

I swallowed the food in my mouth, half-wishing my answer could be yes. "We have to get back so I can get ready for the pre-season. I feel like I haven't thrown in forever, and I need to work out. You know how I get in January."

Being a major league baseball player probably didn't appear like it would be that difficult from the outside. But I worked my ass off for the majority of the year. During the off-season, I still had to work out, stay in shape, and keep myself healthy. Not to mention the fact that I had to start mentally preparing myself for the season months before it actually started, which basically meant I sort of checked out from everything else. Cassie has had to learn to deal with an absentee boyfriend, whether mentally or physically, most of the time. And now I'll be an absentee husband.

"Sucks you're so far away," Dean added before reaching for his glass of orange juice.

"You can come visit us anytime, Dean. Just let us know. We'd love to have you," Cassie said with a smile.

"Thanks, Sis."

"What about me? Can I come visit anytime?" Melissa cocked her head to the side and Cassie rolled her eyes.

"No," she said before laughing. "Of course, dummy. Actually, you and Dean should visit together sometime."

She winked and I seconded the suggestion. "You two should definitely come out together." Dean's shoulders tensed noticeably as a grunt escaped his lips.

Despite how much I razzed him, I wanted to help my brother get the girl. Yesterday I had caught them hooking up before our wedding, and if I could do anything to get them together once and for all, I'd do it. The boy deserved to be happy.

Gran changed the subject before I could ask any more questions. "Speaking of Dean and traveling," she said, "when do you start at the agency?"

"Yeah, bro," I asked as I kicked Dean under the table. "What's up with you and my agents?" My agents, Ryan and Marc, had offered Dean a job at their sports management company as soon as he graduated.

"It's part-time now, but I start full-time at the end of May," he said with a smile.

"What will you be doing exactly?"

"I'll be a junior agent. They're going to teach me the ropes when it comes to dealing with guys like you." He gave a slight head nod in my general direction.

"Good luck with that," Cassie said with a snicker.

"But I'll mostly be researching at first. I'll be looking at new talent for the guys to check out. It's going to be a lot of computer work and apparently I'll be the local contact for any of the players or their families."

"For everything, or just certain things?" Cassie asked.

Dean shrugged. "I don't know yet. I'm sure there will be questions I can't answer, so maybe just helping facilitate their moves if they get traded, or talk about the trade deadlines and stuff."

Warming up to the subject, Cassie asked, "Do the families call a lot?"

"You have no idea," he said, shaking his head. "Not everyone understands the business side of things, so sometimes they get really frustrated. I have to literally explain every single thing to them that they don't quite grasp."

Cassie's eyes grew wide as she inhaled audibly. "I bet those are some fun and long calls."

Dean nodded. "I was on the phone for over two hours the other day with the wife of one of your ex-teammates."

"Who?" I asked.

"One of the outfielders for the D-backs. She was concerned

about him not getting a long-term extension after last season and wanted to know how that would affect his playing time and reaching the full pension package. I had to explain the entire business side of things to her and I think she was still confused. She's obsessed with the pension."

Gramps dropped his fork and it clanged against the table. "Sorry," he said as he picked it up with a funny look on his face. "How many seasons do you have to play before you get the pension?"

"To get full pension benefits, you have to play for ten full seasons."

"What happens if you get hurt before then, or if you can't play all ten?"

Dean sucked in a breath. "Then you only get a partial pension, but it's way more complicated than that. Your contract terms, the number of years you signed for, it all comes into play."

"Oh, enough of this talk. Let's let the kids have some time together before they leave." Gran pushed back from her chair and started collecting her dishes and the plates closest to her.

"Let me help, please?" Cassie asked and Gran swatted at her hand.

"No, dear. You're a newlywed. Go spend your honeymoon with your friends," she said with a wry laugh as we filed out into the living room.

The rest of the afternoon flew by as we hung out with Dean and Melissa. Before I knew it, Cassie was reminding me we needed to pack our things and say our good-byes. I hated leaving, but at least I wouldn't be alone. I'd never be alone again.

Breaking Bones

Cassie

Three Months Later ...

Engrossed in my work, I fiddled with the key that hung from a chain around my neck, my fingers running across the letters that spelled out STRENGTH across the top. Melissa had given it to me after all the drama with the tabloids and mean fans during Jack's first season. The rule of the necklace, she told me, was that I should keep it until I saw someone else who needed the message on the key more than I did. I hated the thought of ever giving that special gift away, but had to admit it was a really clever idea.

Sitting in my cubicle, I pored over photos I had recently shot during my last assignment. Nora, my boss, wanted to submit one picture for a highly respected photography award. But as I looked at them, I realized that I couldn't pick *the* one.

As usual, I'd become emotionally involved on my assignment, and could no longer see the photo for just what it portrayed. I saw the emotions behind it, the meanings that weren't necessarily captured through my lens.

When I looked at the photograph of the elderly man desperately clutching a child covered in dirt and blood, I saw the hundreds of other people in the background just as desperate and dirty who didn't make it into my picture. Just out of view sat houses demolished into piles of debris, and their owners, faces filled with disbelief, digging through the rubble in vain. Several square miles of land that had once held schools, businesses, and homes, were now completely leveled into what could only be described as a war zone. It sounded so cliché, but that description was the most accurate. Mother Nature sometimes brought hell to Earth. And I captured it with my camera.

It was one thing to see devastation on the news or in magazines, but was quite another to walk through the scene and witness the destruction firsthand. There were no words to describe what it was like to feel your feet crunching through the broken glass and debris of what used to be someone's home. Or what you felt as you saw the shock on people's faces as they realized that everything they'd ever held dear had vanished into thin air, or been crushed into particles of dust. I'd never felt as helpless as I did the day an elderly woman admitted to me that all her family photos and heirlooms had been lost, and I could do nothing but watch as she crumpled to her knees in grief. There was such raw and exposed pain in those first few days after a tragedy, that I often found it hard to shoot. It was virtually indescribable to witness, and almost unbearable to live through.

It probably didn't help my career that I didn't enjoy being intrusive. I wasn't the type of photographer who pushed into people's faces, piercing their personal space in hopes of getting the money shot. It didn't bring me joy to photograph the agony of others. After being with them, experiencing it with them, their pain was forever etched in my memory, and I carried it with me wherever I went. I didn't see the sense, or what good it brought, to expose that pain for all to see.

But then at some point during the recovery, something almost magical seemed to happen. You could literally feel the change in the thick and dusty air. The immediate shock had worn off and people in the community came together in the most incredible of ways. There was a sense of family and strength that was humbling to witness. Every. Single. Time. The focus shifted from each individual's loss and transformed into the community's pulling together as a whole to not only survive, but to come back stronger, more resilient, as a more cohesive whole. Experiencing that transformation was in itself worth all the earlier tears and pain.

That was why it had always been my goal on any assignment to look for the beauty amidst all the heartache. Those tiny moments of peace and happiness, like when two friends see each other for the first time after wondering if the other were dead or alive. When panic turned to elation, that was what I wanted to capture. If I could put hope into a photograph where it looked like none existed, I'd have done my job. At least, I'd have done it the way I wanted to.

"Cassie, come in here." My phone buzzed to life with Nora's voice over the intercom.

I pressed the flashing red button and responded, "Be right in." I rose from my desk and glanced around the workspace.

Joey, the guy I had gone on one date with when Jack and I were broken up, moved away a couple of years ago. He got a job offer back in his hometown of Boston and jumped at the opportunity. Jack had wanted to throw a party when he heard that news. Which I never really understood because, really? It wasn't as if Jack ever had any real competition.

The faces in my office may have changed over the last five years, but the pace remained the same. The floor buzzed with energy of creative people working on layout, designs, and editing. I loved my job and I loved living in this city.

I rapped my knuckles against Nora's door before twisting the knob and pushing it open. She waved me over and pointed for me to sit, her phone pressed tightly against her ear. I did as she asked and waited patiently. Ever since I moved to New York to accept the job offer with this magazine, Nora had always had my back. She supported me when Jack and I went through hell with Chrystle's accusations and the backlash that followed. She even offered to do a full spread on our relationship, just to set the record straight.

In the end, we didn't need to go through with the feature spread because Chrystle's ex-best friend Vanessa did all the dirty work for us. Vanessa gave an exclusive interview to the magazine and spilled every detail of Chrystle's plan to use a fake pregnancy to manipulate Jack into marrying her. My reputation got a much needed-boost, and the fans stopped their incessant name-calling and online hatred of me. Actually, the article had proved to be the best publicity for my relationship with Jack, and I had both Nora and Vanessa to thank for that.

"I'll have them for you by the end of the day. Thanks, Bob."

Nora dropped the handset onto the phone base, then leaned back and raised an eyebrow at me. "So, did you choose a photograph yet?"

I winced. "I've narrowed it down to five. That's better than yesterday," I said, thinking back to the thirty pictures I had scattered on the conference room table yesterday afternoon.

"Jesus, Cassie, just pick one! I'm sure they're all brilliant. Hell, take them home to that hot husband of yours and make him choose," she said with a hearty laugh.

My mouth dropped open. "I'm not making Jack pick! He'd probably close his eyes and see which one his finger lands on."

Nora narrowed her eyes at me. "Which is what you're going to have to do if you don't choose one by the end of the day."

"Fine. I'll pick one," I said with a slight huff.

Nora pushed her wire-rimmed glasses up against the bridge of her nose while she stared at me with a smirk on her face.

"What are you up to?" I asked warily. "Why are you looking at me like that?"

Her smirk turned into a full smile. "I need you to photograph an upcoming feature story."

I cocked my head to the side, knowing full well we had other photographers to handle that type of shoot. Each photographer had a specialty. Some excelled at taking indoor studio shots with models, but I wasn't one of them. I worked best with natural light and unconventional settings, pretty much the exact opposite of a posed studio photo. "Like someone local? Who? Why me?"

"Because it's Trina."

Now I was the one smiling. Trina was the one Mets players'

girlfriend who actually talked to me the first season Jack played on the team. When we met, she had been dating Jack's teammate Kyle. She was a model and missed a lot of games due to her travel schedule, but whenever she was there, she was my savior.

"We're shooting Trina? That's amazing! What's the focus of the story?"

Nora waved a dismissive hand in the air. "Something about 'From Models to Moms in Manhattan.' I haven't worked out all the details yet, but she'll be the focus. And she'll only work with you."

As I shook my head in amazement, my mind drifted back to when I'd first met Trina, and the man who became her new husband.

After the fiasco where our driver, Matteo, tried to kiss me and Jack fired him, Jack eventually allowed him to work for us again. In the meantime, Matteo had opened his own car company for exclusive clientele only. Once he began working with us again, Matteo personally only drove and worked for one couple, Jack and me, but his company was rapidly becoming the go-to car service for all the local pro athletes.

Matteo and Trina started dating right after she and Kyle had called it quits. Their wedding ceremony several months later was small, but elegant. Trina claimed the rushed date had to do with Jack's spring training schedule, so that we could attend the wedding, but I knew the real reason was because she didn't want to be showing in her wedding pictures. Matteo also insisted that they be legally married before their baby entered this world. I remember him saying, "I could wait and marry you someday, but I'd much rather marry you today. Someday may never come. Today is already here. Please don't make me wait to make you my wife."

When Trina had told me she and Matteo were getting married, I nervously asked her if she were certain this was what she wanted. I had clearly gained a deep-seated fear of people marrying for the wrong reasons over the last couple of years; whenever I thought back to the situation with Jack and Chrystle, I shuddered. Putting my fears to rest, Trina had informed me that while they didn't plan on having a baby first and a wedding second, she didn't care what order they did things in. They were truly happy and that was all that mattered. And I had to agree because happiness was all I truly wanted for my friends as well.

Nora looked at me over her glasses and raised her eyebrows, obviously waiting for a response.

"The only reason Trina wants to work with me is because if she hates the pictures, she can make me pay for it later," I said with a giggle.

"You'll do great. We'll book a studio with lots of natural light for you, okay?"

I breathed out in relief. "You know me so well."

"I want pictures of her before and after. Make sure you schedule something with her husband after the baby is born so we can show off the happy family."

"No problem. Is that it?"

"Go pick out a damn picture already."

"Fine. But if it sucks and loses, it's your fault." I shot Nora a grin as I pushed out of my chair and headed toward the door.

Back at my desk, I was no closer to choosing a photo than I was an hour ago. Glancing up, I spotted one of our interns walking through the elevator doors, balancing two cardboard trays filled with coffee cups.

"Becca," I shouted and she glanced up, trying not to spill the drinks. "When you get a minute, can you come over here, please?"

She nodded her head as a small smile appeared. Becca was young and still in college, but she had a good eye. And I liked her style.

"Hi, Cassie. You needed me?" Becca sounded nervous and I breathed out a sigh of relief.

"Yes! Thank God you're here. You have a great eye and I love the way you see things. I need to pick a photo to submit for something, but I can't choose. I'm too close to the subject matter. Which one do you like best?"

A giant, toothy grin spread across Becca's youthful face. "I'm honored. Thank you," she said before hovering over the pictures splayed across my desktop.

It took her all of two seconds to grab a photo and declare it was the one. And I trusted her eye because it meant something in that particular picture stood out above all the others.

"Thank you, Becca. You're a lifesaver!"

After work, I stepped through the revolving door and onto the crowded sidewalk. Sidestepping the pedestrian traffic, I weaved my way toward the idling black car at the curb. Matteo stood patiently waiting for me next to the car, just like he did every evening. His handsome face broke out into a wide grin as I neared and he held open the passenger door.

"Why are you so smiley?" I asked and he shrugged.

He hopped into the driver's seat and pulled into traffic. "Life's good, Cassie. Life is good," he said in an annoying singsong voice. Matteo's attitude had been like this ever since he and Trina had hooked up.

"You're so annoying. Go home to your hot wife."

"I will. Right after I drop you off at your hot husband's office," he said playfully with a wink.

"Ew," I said with a shudder. "Don't say Jack's hot and then wink. It's weird."

Unable to respond, he broke out into a huge belly laugh. He was still chortling a little over it as he navigated his way to the field while I scrolled through my personal e-mails on my phone.

A few minutes later, he straightened up and said over his shoulder, "Trina told me about the photo shoot," which got my attention.

I glanced up to meet his eyes in the rearview mirror. "Yeah. It should be great. You're in it too, you know?"

Matteo's posture changed as he shifted nervously in his seat. "I am?"

"Yes. But not until after the baby is born. I'm going to shoot Trina now while she's showing and then all three of you after."

"Just make sure you take the most pictures of her. She's the one who sells magazines, not me," he offered humbly.

I rolled my eyes. "Oh yeah, 'cause being forced to look at your mug is really hard on the ladies," I said with a laugh.

"I knew you wanted me," he teased and I almost choked.

Rolling my eyes, I shook my head and gave a little snort. "Not this again."

Since Jack forgave Matteo, acknowledging his hotness no longer made me feel completely awkward. Granted, I wouldn't be walking around and announcing it to the world anytime soon, but still. It also didn't hurt that Matteo eventually realized that his feelings for me weren't based in reality. He figured out quickly that he had gotten caught up in protecting me and caring about me. It muddled his emotions, but once Trina entered the picture, any romantic feelings he thought he had for me were out the window. Thank God for Trina.

The car slowed to a stop as I gathered my things. Matteo reached for the driver's side handle and I stopped him. "You don't have to let me out. I got it." I opened my own door and scooted out before leaning into the open passenger window, "See you later, future cougar prey."

"Cassie!" Matteo called out in mock indignation as I turned away and walked toward the entry gates of the stadium, laughing. I knew Matteo would love every minute of attention he would get once the article was published.

I scooted into my regular seat next to Tara in the wives' section, my presence here now a familiar sight amongst the other girlfriends, wives, family, and friends. No longer a girlfriend, the players' wives accepted me the way they only accepted other wives. And as much as I hated to admit it, being married changed things. I never planned on treating any of the players' girlfriends the way I was treated, but I acknowledged the difference between being married and not. The social hierarchy existed for a reason, and after seeing the number of girls that came and went with some of these guys, I understood now in a way that had only offended me before.

When I glanced down at the field, the sight of Jack warming up forced my heart to squeeze with pride. His gray sliding pants hugged against the muscles as he lifted his leg into the air before each pitch. The black shirt-style jersey waved in the breeze he created as his arm flew down to release the ball.

I watched as Jack grabbed his hat and tipped it twice, and I couldn't hide my smile. That was his sign to me. He had started doing it when I couldn't travel with him on his road trips, which had become more and more frequent with my work. Whenever he pitched, he'd tip his hat twice and his face would light up with a soft smile. He never knew if the cameras were on him or not, but he tipped his hat regardless.

Eventually it became a habit, because he started doing it at the home games as well. Sometimes his eyes would flash to the stands and meet mine. When they did, I swear my heart would stop beating, causing my breath to catch. Every. Single. Time. If anyone noticed, I would have been embarrassed, but no one ever seemed to.

I more than loved this man. My husband. My ball player.

My Jack Fucking Carter.

Even his name still gets me all hot and bothered.

Jack bent over deeply, looking at the catcher through the glove covering half his face. With a shake of his head, he indicated no to whatever pitch the catcher wanted him to throw. Another shake and the catcher called time out, than ran over to Jack, who stood waiting on the mound, kicking the dirt.

After a short conversation, the catcher gave Jack a pat on the ass before jogging to his position behind home plate. The umpire pointed at Jack and Jack's feet touched the rubber mound. With one fluid motion, the ball left his hand and the batter swung and missed. The ball crashed against the catcher's glove, the sound of it echoing throughout the stadium as the crowd erupted into cheers and I smiled. I loved watching him play. It seemed silly to call Jack beautiful, but when he played baseball … he was.

Someone yelled from the dugout area, but Jack waved them off with his glove hand. I scooted to the edge of my seat and automatically held my breath, anticipating the pitch. Jack leaned down, eyeing the catcher before nodding his head in agreement with the called pitch. He lowered his glove to his waist before bringing it back up in time with the rising of his knee. His entire body lurched forward with the release of the pitch and the crack of the bat meeting the ball distracted everyone else's eyes but mine. My eyes stayed loyally focused on the guy I loved.

Because my eyes never left Jack, I witnessed the entire incident. The ball screamed back at him and he reacted as best he could; his body twisted to get out of the way as his pitching hand instinctively reached out to stop the flying ball. I watched as the ball crashed against Jack's exposed hand before dropping to the ground near his feet.

He scrambled to make the play, but a pained scream tore from his lips as he tried to close his hand around the ball. Face contorted with pain, Jack took a knee and pressed his chin tightly against his chest.

Someone yelled for time out and Jack's manager bolted onto the field. He helped Jack to his feet and walked him out of view.

"Shit," I muttered to myself.

"Go, Cassie," Tara demanded. "Get down to the locker room. That's where they're taking him."

Without a word I nodded, grabbed my things, and hurried toward the staircase that would take me underground. I flew down the last set of stairs to where anyone in the public could go before heading through a private door. Once inside, the air of the cold brick tunnels hit me. The tunnels ran the length of the stadium and unless you'd been under here before, you wouldn't know they existed. I rounded the corner and jogged up toward the burly security guard.

"Hey, Jimmy, is he here? Did you see them bring Jack off the field?" I asked, my voice distraught.

His forehead creased as he answered, "Jack? No. What happened?"

I released a shaky breath. "He hurt his hand."

"Really? Damn. I hope he's okay." He stepped aside, revealing a small clearing between the guardrails, and I rushed through, walking as fast as my nervous legs would allow.

I followed along with the bricks as they curved gently, noticing the Mets sign attached to the wall up ahead. My pace quickened as I ached to reach the double mahogany doors that read NEW YORK METS CLUBHOUSE.

Another security guard sat in a folding chair next to the entrance, his face pinched with concern. He stood upon my approach. "Cassie. He's in there with the doc." The sympathy in his sad eyes rattled me even further, and my mouth went completely dry.

"How did he look, Joe?"

"He was in a lot of pain," he admitted grimly.

My throat constricted, making it hard to swallow. I realized in that moment that I'd never once considered the possibility of Jack getting hurt. He seemed invincible in a way … like his body was born to play this sport and it would never allow him to be hurt by it. It would never betray him like that.

But it did.

And I found myself scared to death about what this meant for him. Jack without baseball … well, that wasn't Jack at all. I wouldn't even know who that person was; I'd never known Jack when baseball wasn't a huge part of his life. Worry shot through me and I couldn't stop a nervous shiver.

"Cassie?" Joe's voice echoed in the tunnel, followed by the sound of him hanging up the rotary phone. Unable to speak, I looked up at him helplessly. "No one else is in there," he said gently. "You can go in."

He opened one of the large doors for me and I walked through into the one place at the stadium I'd never been before. I eyed the oversized couch and the carpet patterned with the team's logo, before my gaze fell on the lockers bearing each player's name and jersey number, a soft spotlight highlighting each one as if they were museum exhibits. I laughed to myself that the guys called them "lockers" when they looked more like the thin oak closets you would find in hotel rooms.

I found myself longing to photograph the room as each individual detail called to me in ways that only new places can. Occupational habit, I supposed. Or denial, maybe.

"Kitten?" Jack's voice rang out through the large space, an undertone of pain causing it to sound different somehow.

Snapped back to the present, I called out, "Jack? Where are you?"

"Walk to the back of the room and make a right."

As I hurried past the row of lockers, number 23 grabbed my attention and I couldn't resist the impulse to pause for just a second at Jack's locker since I'd never seen it, and might never have the chance again. His travel bag and street clothes hung inside, waiting for him, and I ran my fingers down the fabric, moving them slightly. Taped against the back wall was a picture of the two of us on our wedding day, flanked by other candid shots of us. I loved how much this man displayed his love for me.

With a slight smile, I headed toward the back of the room and rounded the corner just as the team doctor injected a shot into Jack's arm to help ease his pain. I noticed that he didn't even wince.

"I think it's shattered," Jack admitted as soon as his dark brown eyes met mine.

SHATTERED.

And in that moment, that's exactly how my heart felt. I rushed to his side, needing to be as physically close to him in that moment as I could.

"We don't know that yet," the doctor interjected. "I'm Dr. Evans."

I extended my hand to his. "I'm Cassie."

One look at Jack's face and my chest ached with the need to protect and comfort him. I stroked his shoulder as I asked, my tone all business, "What do we know?"

"It's definitely broken, but to what extent I'm not sure yet."

I shrugged my shoulders. "But it will heal just fine, right? People break their hands all the time."

Dr. Evans nodded. "True. But we need to make sure it won't require surgery, or pins or metal plates."

Pins or metal plates? Oh my God.

Jack swallowed audibly and I continued to prod the doctor, my growing concern overruling all levelheadedness. "And if it does, then what? People have surgery on their hands all the time too. They get better."

"Yes, Mrs. Carter, they do," he said with a frown. "But most of those people aren't major league pitchers."

My heart sank. "So, what are you saying?"

"I'm saying that I need to x-ray his hand first and then I'll have more answers for you."

Jack's chin dropped to his chest and I watched his eyes

close.

"Do I need to take him to a hospital?" I started to reach for my cell phone to call Matteo.

"No, no. I have a machine in the other room. As the team's physician, I'm responsible for Jack's condition and his recovery. It's my job."

"Wow. So we don't have to go anywhere else?" Since I'd never thought this through, I didn't know how it worked when a major league player was injured. Wrongly, I'd assumed Jack would have to get checked out at regular hospital, like normal people. But then again, the team chartered their own commercial planes to fly them places, so nothing about this lifestyle was normal.

"If I'm on the road with the team, one of my trainers will be here to help you, so no. You should never have to take Jack anywhere other than here."

The Mets organization cared about Jack's recovery, so I allowed myself to be comforted by the thought that he would be taken care of by the people who were invested in him the most. It was in their best interest, as well as his, to get him healed.

"If you'll excuse us, Mrs. Carter, we'll only be a minute." The doctor motioned for Jack to follow him into another room. "Let's go see what we're dealing with, Jack."

I paced the floor, one hand tugging at my lips from nervous habit. I wanted to call Dean, but knew he'd ask me questions I didn't have the answers to. So I waited to call anyone until I had more to tell them. A broken hand was one thing, but having a hand that required surgery was another.

A few minutes later, Jack exited the medical room alone

and scooped me into a careful hug. I felt his heart racing as our chests pressed together. "I love you, Kitten." He gave me a quick kiss, then released me and hopped back onto the exam table. His hand looked painful, his fingers had taken on a purplish tint and were swollen to a ridiculous size. The sight of it made my stomach tighten painfully and I had to turn my gaze away.

"I love you too." I wanted to say more, but words failed me. Bringing my hand toward my heart, my fingers grazed across the ball chain necklace that lay there. I glanced down at the key attached and moved my fingers to it, rubbing them across the etched letters for comfort.

Between the lies from Chrystle and the brutality from the press and fans, it wasn't that long ago when I felt like my insides were unraveling. Melissa had given me this necklace when I needed it the most. Imagining that Jack was experiencing the same sort of feelings right about now, I realized this was the right time to pass the necklace on, as was intended.

I reached around the back of my neck, my fingers gripping at the chain before pulling it over my head. When I lowered the necklace around Jack's neck, he looked up at me, his face pale and strained with pain, and raised his eyebrows at me. The bronze key fell against his sweaty white T-shirt before he glanced down at it. With his uninjured hand, he lifted the key and flipped it to the stamped side, then read its message out loud. "Strength."

"You need this more than I do," I said before leaning in and planting a kiss on his scruffy cheek. "We'll get through this. No matter what the doctor says when he walks through that door, we'll get through this."

I tried to sound positive and strong, but my insides were rattled and fraying. If Jack lost baseball because of this, I wasn't sure he'd ever get over it. His self-image, his hopes and dreams—hell, his whole identity—were wrapped up in the game. If the worst happened, if he could never play again, I had no idea how he'd process that loss.

The sound of the door creaking open caused me to pull my gaze from Jack's and glance behind me. Footsteps slapped against the floor as Dr. Evans walked in our direction, a smile on his face. "Good news. You don't need surgery and it's not shattered." I exhaled a huge sigh of relief and watched Jack do the same as the doctor continued. "You do have multiple fractures, however, here and here." He pointed at areas on the x-rays as Jack tensed beside me. "And we need to get you in a cast immediately."

"How long will I be out?" Jack asked, his face turning even whiter.

"Minimum, six weeks. It could have been a lot worse. Frankly, I'm surprised it isn't."

I watched as Jack flexed his jaw and worked to keep his emotions in check. He didn't like that answer, but there was no answer that Jack would have liked. One day not playing baseball was one day too many for him. Six weeks probably sounded like a death sentence.

"I can't leave my team for that long." Jack shook his head as he mumbled, "I can't let them down like that."

"Jack, look at me," I begged. "You're not letting them

down. They'll understand, and they'll want you to get better. Six weeks is better than six months, right? Let's take it one day at a time."

The pained look in his eyes informed me that these next six weeks were going to be anything but easy.

I'm a Baseball Player

Jack

Hearing Dr. Evans tell me I'd be out for six weeks made me want to fucking scream. But I didn't scream when I was frustrated; I hit shit. And right now, with a broken fucking hand, I couldn't hit anything.

A million thoughts raced through my head at once.

Why the fuck did I stick my hand out like that? No one in their right mind could catch a fast-ball being hit straight back at them. I must be mental. What if my hand doesn't heal right? What if they find someone new to replace me? Six weeks is a long time to have your job up for grabs. What if I can't throw again after this? I didn't want to get hurt. I just want to play baseball. What if I can't play anymore? I busted my ass to get where I am, I don't want to lose it. I'm a ball player, that's what I am. That's who I am. What the hell will I do if I'm not playing baseball?

It was one thing when it was your choice to leave the only

job in this world you could see yourself doing, but being forced to quit was another. The truth was that it was rarely ever your choice to leave.

I sucked in a breath, took one look at my beautiful wife, and hopped off the table. Grabbing her by the hand, I pulled her forcefully out of the locker room.

"Jesus, Jack, stop. That hurts." She jerked her hand from my grip and I winced.

"Sorry, Kitten. I just want to get out of here."

She looked at me with sympathy in her eyes and I almost fucking exploded. The last thing I needed right now was my wife looking at me with pity. "Don't look at me like that," I ordered.

"Like what?" She stopped walking and tilted her head at me questioningly.

"Like my life just ended and you want to make sure I'm going to be okay."

She huffed out a breath before rolling her green eyes at me. "You're an idiot."

"Excuse me?" I shouted, my voice echoing throughout the concrete tunnels.

"Of course I want to make sure you're okay, Jack! Jesus. Excuse me for giving a shit about your mental state. But I never once thought that your life just ended."

"You don't get it," I breathed out, my tone agitated. I was acting like a complete asshole in this moment and I fucking knew it. But I was pissed off. I was angry about putting my hand out like that ... for letting it get hit ... for letting it get broken.

"Oh, so now I don't get it? You're joking, right?" she snapped in response, her tone matching my own, before she turned around and walked away from me.

Fuck.

I needed to stop doing this to her; it wasn't fair. Irritated with myself, I smacked the palm of my hand against my head before rushing to catch up to her. I reached for her arm with my good hand, desperately pulling for her to stop. "Kitten. I'm sorry. I'm mad at myself, not you."

She nodded, her long blonde hair swinging with the motion, then let out a little sigh. "I know." Then she locked her fingers with mine and pulled me toward the parking lot.

Once in the car with Matteo behind the wheel, I watched Cassie as she scrolled through her contacts, searching for my brother's phone number. She must have already warned Matteo, because he hadn't said two words to me and was avoiding all eye contact. My girl was good at this. I wished I hadn't been such a dick earlier.

I reached my free hand across the seat and squeezed her thigh. She glanced at me, still a little wary of me, it seemed. "Thank you," I whispered as she scrunched up her face in confusion.

"For what?" She scooted her body closer to mine to keep our conversation private.

"You know what." I nodded my head in Matteo's direction

and she shrugged. I chose wisely when it came to picking a wife. She was the best thing I'd ever done. I needed to not fuck us up. Again.

She refocused her attention to her phone and I watched as Dean's name popped up on her screen and she pressed SEND. The phone rang twice before my brother's voice came from the speaker. "What's up, Sis?"

Cassie turned off the speaker and sucked in a breath as she lifted the phone to her ear. "Hey, Dean. I just wanted to let you know before you saw it on *SportsCenter* or *Baseball Tonight* or something." She paused briefly before continuing. "Jack broke his hand tonight."

I could only imagine the questions my brother was shooting at her from the other end of the line. His voice was muffled since she'd taken him off speaker, so I couldn't make out any of his words.

"He was pitching and the ball got hit straight back at him. He threw his hand up to stop it, or catch it, or something. But the ball crashed into it and he has multiple fractures."

Cassie grew silent and I knew Dean was talking her ear off. I glanced in the rearview mirror and noticed Matteo paying attention to Cassie's side of the conversation as well.

"Don't think you're getting a vacation or anything, buddy," I called out in his direction.

"Wouldn't dream of it," he responded without missing a beat.

"I still have to go to the field every day to work out and I'll need a ride there and back," I informed him with a smirk.

"I'll have to check with my other clients." He raised his

eyebrows and looked at Cassie. "But tell me, do you still have to go to the games and stuff?"

I nodded. "Yep. I have to suit up for the home games and hang out in the dugout."

"What about when they're on the road?"

"I meet with a trainer at the field when the team's gone."

"So you won't travel with them then?"

"Nope. Not for six weeks." I sighed, suddenly feeling agitated.

Cassie sounded like she was wrapping things up. "Yeah. I'll call you tomorrow. Will you let Gran and Gramps know for us?" She paused. "Thank you so much. Yep, I'll tell him. 'Bye."

She pressed END and turned toward me. "Dean says to take it easy and to not do anything stupid."

"What the hell would I possibly do?"

"I have no idea. He's your brother," she teased and I grabbed at her.

"Oh yeah? Well, he's your brother too," I reminded her and a smile appeared across her face as she turned away from me. I leaned over and grazed my teeth against her earlobe, touching it with the tip of my tongue before whispering, "I love your smile. It's sexy. Really fucking sexy. Don't be mad at me. I really am sorry."

Her face turned and I pressed my lips against hers before she could respond. Her lips parted slightly as she gave a little gasp that sent a message straight to my groin, so I sucked on her bottom lip lightly, then swept my tongue across it before sliding it into her mouth. The throbbing of my dick replaced the throbbing in my hand as I realized I had the cure to any broken bones right here in this car with me.

My hot-as-hell wife.

Matteo cleared his throat. "Uh. We're here, horny teenagers."

Cassie squeaked and I laughed as we pulled out of our kiss. "Thanks, cock-block." I eyed him before opening the car door. "I'll call you when I know my schedule for the next couple of weeks, okay?"

He nodded. "Sounds good."

We walked into our apartment building and straight onto the waiting elevator. The doors closed and I pinned Cassie against the wall.

"Jack, what are—"

"Be quiet," I demanded before quieting her with my mouth. I nipped at her lips before exploring her neck. My unbroken hand followed the curves of her waist, down her hips, before cupping her ass. I squeezed, causing her to whimper, and my dick felt like it might explode right there. I needed to be in her. And I needed it now.

The ding of the elevator arriving on our floor interrupted the sexual assault I was launching on Cassie's irresistible mouth. I moved to grab her with my broken hand and quickly switched arms. Reaching for her, I pulled a little too aggressively toward me and she yanked her hand from mine.

I didn't apologize. Instead I fumbled with the keys, constantly reminding myself to do everything with the opposite hand. You never realize how much you take for granted until you're forced to. My left hand had always been great, completely reliable, my go-to hand ... until it broke and stopped working. Now I had to remember to perform even the most mundane of tasks with the hand that felt the most foreign to me.

Fighting off the frustration that seemed to be making itself at home, I needed to do something that made me feel like a man. Finally managing to get the front door open, I moved to grab Cassie, but she pressed her hands against my chest to stop me.

"Jack? Aren't we going to talk about this?"

"Talk about what?"

"Your hand? What you're thinking?"

I huffed out a laugh. "Yeah, Kitten. We'll talk. After you give me what I want, I'll give you what you want."

I needed to fuck my wife. I needed to own her, take her, show her I was still the man in this relationship, even if I wasn't the man on the field. Her eyes narrowed as her lips twisted into a snarl. My girl was itching for a fight, and I wanted to suck that expression right off her face.

"That's not how it works, jackass," she snapped, and I immediately puffed out my chest.

"Don't play tough with me. You know you want some of this." I ran my hand down the length of my body and she chuckled. "So now my body's funny to you? I'll show you funny."

I stormed into the living room before stopping at one of the many mason jars filled with quarters around our house. Remembering the quarters I'd saved for our first date after Cassie told me it cost me fifty cents every time I touched her, I smiled to myself. She had tried to be so sassy, but I saw her defenses weaken when I poured the bag of quarters all over the table at the diner where we were having dinner. Holding two coins between my unbroken fingers, I walked back to where Cassie stood. She hadn't moved. Not a muscle. She wanted this as much as I did, no matter how much she pretended she didn't.

"Open your hands." She eyed me, but refused to move. "I said, open your hands, Kitten."

She slowly cupped her hands in front of her body, and I dropped the fifty cents into her palms.

"Now, get in the bedroom."

Being Hurt Doesn't Work For Us

Cassie

Ever since we left the field, Jack had been a roller coaster of emotions, taking me on a violently jerky ride. One minute he was sweet and attentive, and rude and nasty the next. Unsure of which Jack I might get, I stayed quiet in our bed in the aftermath of having sex, trying to figure out what the hell had just happened between us.

Jack had always dominated in the bedroom, but this was something else entirely. He bossed me around, making demands he'd never once said out loud before. He pushed and pulled at my body like he owned it, and I had no choice but to comply. Maybe under different circumstances I might have been turned on by his aggression, but not like this. Not after my husband just broke his pitching hand and potentially ended his career. He wasn't in his right mind and his performance in the bedroom only proved it.

I'd never in a thousand years tell him that the thought of his career being over crossed my mind, but it did. Of course it did. I wasn't an idiot. Multiple fractures would eventually heal, but there could be complications. Everyone knew that. Jack needed his hand to work on the ball field. His fingers were required to grip and maneuver across the seams of the baseball for different pitches. If his grip loosened, his pitches wouldn't be the same. And the idea of Jack without baseball scared the hell out of me.

I knew he avoided talking about his injury for this very reason. I wasn't the only one scared, but at least I admitted it. Glancing over at his sweaty body, the lines of his chest rising and falling with each breath, I longed to make his pain and hurt go away. He was quieter than he'd ever been before, and I realized how deep in his own head he must be.

Although I was the queen of building emotional walls, Jack could do a pretty good job too if he wanted. The memory of how I'd behaved earlier in our relationship flooded through me. All the times I kept my feelings to myself, refusing to burden him with any of my personal drama. The only problem was that not talking to Jack about it forced me into personal overload, where the only solution I saw was to run away. Holding feelings in hadn't worked then, and it wouldn't work now. Desperate to keep the lines of communication open between us, I touched his chest lightly. "Jack?" I whispered, still reeling from the sex we'd just experienced.

He rolled over to face me. "Yep?" His tone sounded annoyed again.

"I just wanted to talk about how you're feeling, what you're thinking, something?"

He growled. "Cassie, can we not do this tonight, please? Can't you just give me one fucking night to process everything before you make me spill my guts like a fucking chick?"

I fought against the tears threatening to spill over and rolled away from his glare. "But you said we could talk after."

"Yeah? Well, I fucking lied. Just go to sleep."

Suddenly I felt very small. I definitely wasn't used to this Jack and I most certainly didn't like it. He had never acted so callous when it came to talking to me before. He seemed so uncaring, so cold. My brain knew it was all a front, but my heart couldn't take the pain. Being treated like this by Jack, of all people, hurt more than words. We were married now. Didn't he feel differently about us? I certainly did. Or I had up until about five minutes ago.

Wiping the tears I couldn't stop from falling, I silently made a deal with myself to give him time to process and deal with what happened tonight, but after that he needed to get his act together. I wouldn't put up with this attitude forever, and I'd make that abundantly clear if necessary.

I woke up the following morning to the light streaming through the windows where I forgot to close the curtains the night before. It was stupid the things you forgot to do when you were otherwise occupied with situations you weren't expecting. Sucking in a small breath, I glanced at Jack, who appeared to be sleeping peacefully on his back, his cast-covered arm resting across his bare chest.

Pushing myself up from the mattress, I walked quietly toward the bathroom to get ready for work.

"Cassie, can you close the fucking curtains?" Jack's sharp voice cut through me.

Apparently a good night's sleep had done nothing for his attitude. Honest to God, no matter how beautiful I thought this man was, there was no way I would deal with this craptitude for very long. He was testing my patience, and that was something I had in short supply anyway. Fighting the urge to snap back at him, call him names, or stand up for myself, I merely did as he requested before walking into the bathroom and closing the door behind me. I stared at my reflection for a good five minutes before I attempted to do a single thing to my hair or face.

He'll get past this.

He has to.

Right?

Sucking in a long, deep breath, I closed my eyes and willed myself to be strong. With a firm nod to the only person in the room, I reached for my makeup bag and tossed the contents onto the counter before putting my face on.

When I arrived home from work that evening, Jack wasn't there. I had completely forgotten that the Mets had one last home game before they headed out on the road for ten days. Jack didn't mention anything about attending the game, but I knew he was required to be there. I clicked our television on just to make sure. No sooner had the picture cleared when I heard the announcer talking about Jack's "busted hand" and his face appeared across my high-definition screen. He looked miserable.

By the time Jack got home, I could barely keep my eyes open. When I heard the front door open, I pretended to need a glass of water from the kitchen.

"How was the game?" I asked, trying to sound cheerful and supportive. Jack didn't answer my question. He barely gave me a passing glance before moving around me and into our bedroom.

His silence stunned me.

I stood alone in the kitchen, my bare feet pressing against the cold tile flooring as I clutched at my chest. As soon as the stunned feeling arose, it disappeared. Anger replaced it and I shouted from where I stood, "You gonna pretend like you didn't hear me?" I waited for a response before shouting again, "Are you seriously not talking to me?"

Silence.

I wasn't sure what was worse, the silent treatment or the asshole one. At least when he was being an asshole, he was talking. Not that it was pleasant.

The silent treatment went on for two more days.

Two. More. Days.

When you're living in that sort of hell, two days might as well be years. It felt like a fucking lifetime because I was so goddamned miserable. It affected everything in my life from the second my eyes opened, to the moment my mind finally allowed me to sleep at night. I was consumed by Jack's behavior and the fact that I couldn't get through to him.

I stared at the telephone on my desk and stopped myself from calling to check on Jack at least ten times. Part of me couldn't handle the idea that he'd send my call to voice mail without a second thought. I glanced at my engagement ring and wedding band, suddenly nervous that what we'd just shared with our family and friends felt threatened. Certainly we'd been through tougher relationship challenges than this?

Hadn't we?

I hated the thoughts spinning in my mind, but what if Jack's baseball career were over? Was this how my husband was going to act from here on out, snappy and pissed off all the time? I knew I wouldn't be able to deal with it forever, no matter how much I loved him. I wanted my husband back.

Nora interrupted my musings by calling me into her office to discuss Jack's latest issue. "Close the door," she demanded before I'd even finished walking through it.

With a click, the door closed and I walked to the chair facing her and sat. I laughed as she glared at me, her mouth pursed into a displeased pucker.

"Broke his hand, huh? I bet he's a joy to live with right now." She tapped her pen against a yellow notepad.

"Yeah, he's a real peach. How'd you know?" I asked, wondering how she could be so aware of Jack's moodiness.

"Jack's one of those guys. A real man's man, if you know what I mean. Can't imagine he enjoys feeling helpless. And I'll tell you, Cass, that's exactly how he's feeling right now."

"You're absolutely right, but it sucks. He's acting like a complete jerk." I pulled my mouth into a pout, wanting sympathy or understanding or something.

Her head tipped to one side as a slight smile crept across her lips. "Of course he is. He doesn't know what else to do. He doesn't know *who* else he is if he isn't a baseball player. The bottom line," she paused before looking me straight in the eyes. "He's scared. He may never admit it, but he's terrified of losing the game."

The reality sank into my throat and I swallowed it whole. "I know that. But it doesn't give him the right—"

She clicked her tongue to stop me midsentence. "No, it doesn't give him the right to treat you badly. But just give him some time."

"Don't you have an assignment in another country you can send me on?" I suggested with a halfhearted laugh.

"No, I do not," she said sternly. "And even if I did, I wouldn't send you."

"Why are you out to get me?" I said it half-jokingly, but part of me wondered why she was being so hard on me.

Nora leveled her gaze to mine, a stray wisp of hair falling

over one eye. "I'm not out to get you. I simply refuse to help you run away when it comes to this. He will get past it. And you'll be there for him when he does. You just need to be patient with him right now."

"It's not really my strong suit," I said. "Patience, I mean."

"Honey, you're a woman. You can do anything. And you will." She smiled and waved her hand in dismissal. "Now, get out of here and send me something pretty to look at. These new photographers don't have your eye."

Without another word, I left Nora's office and headed back to my desk. Like I'd done a million times already today, I checked both my cell phone and my work phone; neither showed signs of any missed calls. I hated living like this.

But Nora was right. I could do this. Jack would do this for me, wouldn't he? Hell, I didn't know what Jack would do at this point anymore.

I assumed Jack would still be on vocal strike when I got home from work, so I didn't bother to acknowledge him when I walked through our front door and saw him watching TV in our living room.

"Cassie, bring me a beer."

I froze in our foyer; stopped walking, moving, breathing. "Oh, now you're talking to me?" I belted out, still surprised by his demanding tone.

His disheveled head turned in my direction. "What the hell

are you talking about?"

My temper hit the boiling point as I tossed my purse and keys on the hallway table and stalked to the living room. Hands on hips, I shouted, "Are you fucking delusional or something? Do you even realize that you haven't spoken to me in almost three days?"

Jack glanced back at me from his usual TV-viewing spot on the leather sofa, his cast-covered arm resting on a throw pillow and his sock-covered feet propped on the ottoman. I watched as his eyebrows pulled together before slowly releasing. "You're exaggerating," he said flatly. "Beer me." Then he turned his focus back on the Mets versus Astros game on the television.

Tempted to pull a beer from the fridge and chuck it at his fucking head, I stormed through the kitchen before heading toward our bedroom. "Get off your ass and get it yourself," I shouted as I slammed the door shut.

Angry tears burned at the back of my eyes and I wanted to scream and throw things. I felt like a prisoner in my own home. Whatever room Jack was in, I wanted to be nowhere near it, his rejection hurt me so badly. But the tears wouldn't fall; I was too busy feeling pissed off to waste time crying. Grabbing my latest read, I sank against my pillows and cracked open the spine, wanting nothing more than to escape the hell our life had become for just a little while.

"Stop acting like a bitch," Jack shouted through the closed door as he stomped through the kitchen.

My head snapped up. Did he just call me a bitch? Jack had never talked that way to me before. Ever. I slammed my book down on the bedside table and dialed the only person I thought could help me. The phone rang five times and I almost hung up when I heard his winded voice say, "Hello?"

"Dean?" I paused.

"What's up, Sis?"

I smiled, the action feeling almost alien after the last few days. "Are you busy? Is this a bad time?" I listened as he struggled for breath.

"No, it's fine. I just had to run upstairs."

"Do you think you could come out here for a little bit? I know you're busy with work, but even if it's just for a few days it would be great. I need your help with Jack."

He laughed a breathy sound into the phone. "Is he really that bad?"

"Let's just say we're not really seeing eye to eye right now, so maybe you should come out here and punch him in one."

He snorted. "I'll gladly beat the shit out of him. So, what's he doing?"

"Dean," my tone turned serious. "He literally hasn't spoken a single word to me in almost three days. Not. A. Word," I said, pausing between each word for effect.

"Say what? You're joking." Dean half laughed.

My frustration boiling over, I balled my hand into a fist and punched my thigh. "I'm not joking. It's not funny. I need your help."

"Okay, sorry. I can't believe he's being like that," he said. "I mean, I can. But I can't believe he's being like that to *you*."

"Yeah, it's pretty awful," I admitted.

"You let me know when you want me there, and I'm there."

I breathed out in relief. "Thank God. I'll take care of all the details. Just e-mail me your schedule and I'll do my best to book around it."

"Ryan and Marc will let me take off whatever time I need. Book whatever and I'll be there."

"Thank you so much, Dean. I'll see you soon." I ended the call, then got up and opened the bedroom door and walked out into the darkening house.

When I switched on the kitchen light, I heard, "Finally come out to get me that beer?" Jack's voice broke into the room, cutting the sliver of hope that was weaving its way within me clean through.

I bit my tongue so hard it almost bled. I wanted to be the bigger person, but he made it really damned hard.

At my silence, he called out, "Who knew it was that hard to get your broken husband a beer?" He was relentless.

"For Pete's sake, Jack, you're not broken. It's not like you can't get up and get it yourself." I leaned on the kitchen table and breathed deeply, willing myself to stay calm.

"I am broken!" he shouted, his eyes turning around to meet mine, the fire in them blazing. "You think I don't know what you think of me?"

What?

I stood in the small space between our room and the kitchen, stunned at his outburst. I honestly had no idea what Jack was talking about, and wasn't sure how to respond without this turning even uglier than it had already been.

His gorgeous face twisted into a sneer. "See? You can't even admit it! At least say it to my face."

"Jack," I said carefully. "I honestly have no idea what

you're talking about." I shifted my weight uncomfortably from one foot to the other.

"Don't lie to me, Cassie. The least you can do is not lie to me." His voice took on a desperate quality and it caused my heart to ache for him, the pain so real I was certain it could be seen on an EKG.

Turning to face Jack where he still sat on the couch, I let out a sigh and my shoulders slumped. "I'm not lying to you, Jack. I love you." I longed to cross the space between us and close it, wrap my arms around him and reassure him that it would all be okay, but I was too scared. I couldn't make him that kind of promise and we both knew it.

Emotions flitted across his face—yearning, distrust, then his expression settled into an angry mask. "But it's not enough to love me when I'm broken like this, right? You love a baseball player, not just a man. And I'm not a baseball player anymore. I'm worthless on the field and I'm worthless at home. I know that's what you think. And I don't blame you, but at least admit it."

My heart twisted as I looked at the torment evident on his face. I wanted so desperately to lock that pain and insecurity in a box, and then burn that box to ash and dust so he'd never feel this way again. Seeing my confident husband reduced to this shell of a man crushed me.

I stepped toward him and he snapped, "Don't! Don't come over here and look at me with pity in your eyes. Don't pity me, Cassie! I don't deserve your pity. And I don't want it. Just leave me the fuck alone."

"That's enough!" I cried out with a sob. "I can't do this

anymore!" Clutching one hand to my mouth, I broke down, tears of frustration falling without warning.

Jack narrowed his eyes and spit out, "I knew it! I knew you were weak."

His voice burned me like venom from a snake bite, and I steadied my shaking body against the counter.

He doesn't mean it.

He doesn't mean it.

He doesn't mean it.

It was easy for your head to know the truth, but try telling that to your heart when it was too busy shattering to hear.

Trembling, whether from heartbreak or anger, I wasn't sure, I swiped at my wet cheeks and said, "I just meant that I can't deal with your attitude anymore. Dean is coming out here, so you'd better get your act together."

I'd wondered how I was going to tell Jack that Dean was coming out. Thankfully, he'd just given me the perfect opportunity.

"What the hell do you mean, Dean is coming out here? When did you two plan this little bullshit charade?" he demanded, slamming his unopened beer down on our coffee table.

He'd already gotten himself a beer? What the hell?

"Today. I can't deal with you like this, Jack. You're mean. You're just plain mean."

His good hand balled into a fist before he looked away. "Don't know what you think bringing Dean out here is going to do."

"Yeah, me either." I sighed before walking away. It seemed

like that's all I did lately, walk away from him instead of to him. I wondered if he truly thought I was quitting, or giving up. It probably looked that way in his eyes. But the truth was, I just needed to leave him alone, give him space before I said something I'd regret. We were clearly making each other miserable, and I didn't want to make it any worse. Being away from him was the only way I could think of to stop the fighting.

Welcome to the
Big Apple

Cassie

Tapping my foot, I waited in baggage claim at JFK for Melissa and Dean. Tempted to bring a super-embarrassing fake sign congratulating them on the birth of their sextuplets, I'd nixed that idea and waited empty-handed instead, an anxious smile plastered all over my face. Melissa's head covered with bouncy curls appeared first, followed by Dean's muscular frame towering over her.

When Melissa caught wind of Dean's impending trip, she invited herself along, claiming she still hadn't seen our place yet and it wasn't fair if Dean saw it first. Even though she'd been to New York a hundred times before, it had been years since she'd last visited. I said yes immediately, but reminded them both that we only had one guest room, so no fighting over the bed and the couch. In the end, they each agreed to share the one bed and I secretly wondered if I could cast a love spell on it before they arrived. I might have even searched for one online.

Hell, I think we were all tired of waiting for the inevitable coupling that should be Dean and Melissa. But maybe it was just inevitable to all of us on the outside? Especially since no one really knew what had happened between them.

Melissa looked around curiously as she grabbed me with both hands. "No Jack?" she asked and I breathed out a sarcastic sound.

Dean eyed me with sympathy. "I'll kick his ass, Sis. It's all good." Then he wrapped his strong arms around me and gave me a tight squeeze.

I shook my head. "It's definitely not all good, Dean. It's not even close to *all good*."

The three of us walked side by side toward the baggage claim carousel. "Is it that bad?" Melissa asked in a low voice.

I nodded. "I've never seen this side of him." Unable to compare Jack's current personality to any of his moods I'd witnessed since knowing him, I turned to Dean. "Has he ever been like this before?"

Dean shrugged. "Not that I can think of. I mean, he was a wreck when he lost you, but he wasn't a dick. The things you've been telling me don't sound like my brother at all."

His words actually relieved me. "I was hoping you'd say that."

"Why?"

"Because then this isn't really a part of him, you know? It's just something he's going through right now." I nodded to myself before continuing. "And I think I can deal with that if I know for certain it's eventually going to come to an end."

"Well then, you'd better pray he can pitch in six weeks."

The truth of that sentence sucked the air from my lungs and I almost doubled over in the middle of the airport. Dean was right. And even though I wasn't the type of person who prayed, I would definitely start praying tonight.

We stopped walking as other people from their flight started filling in the space around us. Melissa looked around. "Any paparazzi follow you here?"

I smiled. "They've backed off since the article with Vanessa came out. You know that. Although I am a little surprised they aren't more up my ass since Jack got hurt."

"Be thankful."

"Oh, trust me, I am. The last thing I need is for them to catch wind of Jack's piss-and-vinegar attitude."

Melissa glanced around. "So, where's our hot driver? Meow," she said playfully, raising her eyebrows as I smacked her shoulder.

"He's home with his pregnant wife, you whore. She wasn't feeling well and I told him I'd go with another driver."

"Well, that's no fun." Her bow-shaped lips puckered into that famous Meli pout.

I glanced at Dean, who tried to pretend like her words didn't bother him, but his body language said otherwise. His back had stiffened and his lips had pressed together into a slight snarl. Glancing back at Melissa, I asked, "Who needs Matteo when you have Dean?"

Dean glanced at me, a sarcastic smirk replacing the snarl. "We all know I'm not good enough for Princess Melissa here." He waved his hand in her direction.

"What?" Melissa snapped back. "Whoever said you weren't

good enough for me? And don't call me Princess!"

Tension practically crackled in the air between them, and I sighed.

Dean squinted his hazel eyes and lowered his face to hers. "If you actually liked me back, *Princess*, then we'd be together right now."

She rolled her eyes. "We are together right now, dummy."

"No. I mean we'd be a couple and you know it. Stop avoiding the subject."

"I'm not avoiding anything. You've never even asked," Melissa half-shouted over the sound of the baggage claim carousel kicking into gear.

"Asked? Asked you what? I don't even know what the hell you're talking about right now!" Dean threw his hands into the air before pacing back and forth. "You make me crazy, you know that?"

Melissa shrugged her slim shoulders. "I don't even do anything."

He stopped pacing and pointed a finger at her. "You don't even do anything? YOU DON'T EVEN DO ANYTHING?" he repeated as his face reddened.

"That's what I said." She looked at me before smiling and flipping her hair.

Listening to this verbal ping-pong match all weekend was going to be the death of me. I stepped between them and gritted out, "Holy shit, you two, shut up. Work it out in the bedroom. Please, for the love of all that's holy … just work it out."

"I've been trying for the last two years," Dean said through gritted teeth.

"He always makes me the bad guy!" Melissa yelled before stomping away.

Dean's hands flew to the back of his head, where he threaded his fingers through his hair. "She is going to fucking kill me. Look at her."

I did as he asked and stifled a laugh. Melissa was currently struggling to get her suitcase off the spinning carousel. The damn thing looked twice her size and she was being dragged along as she yanked at it, unable to maneuver it over the edge and onto the floor.

"Come on, let's get out of here." I nudged his rib cage with my shoulder.

When we got into the car, I positioned myself in the rear seat between Dean and Melissa, feeling like a referee just waiting to blow my whistle and shout, "Interference!" or "Offside!" But neither of them so much as looked at the other. This was going to be a long few days.

Dean stared out the car window, his eyes widening as he took in the views. I remembered how alive I felt the first time I came here. In the midst of my Jack-shattered heart, New York seemed to be the only place that could mend it. It buzzed with energy in the day, but it created it at night. I loved this city.

"Wait until you see the view from our balcony."

Dean turned to me. "I can't believe you guys live here."

"It's pretty awesome, right?" I smiled.

"I've never seen anything like it."

The car slowed to a stop as we pulled in front of our building. "We're here."

Dean didn't wait for our driver to open his door. "This looks like something straight out of Disneyland," he said, glancing up at the light bulbs that lined the awning over our building's entrance, and I laughed.

"It's just those lights. I know. They look like the movie theater on Main Street. But you won't think that in the daytime. Come on."

"Thanks, Pete." I smiled at the driver as he unloaded the last of the suitcases from the trunk.

Melissa looked straight up into the night sky. "Twenty-three floors up, right?"

"Yep," I responded before wrapping an arm around her. "It's not that bad. Just don't look down." A small sound squeaked out of my best friend.

The doorman held open the front door for us to walk through. "Evening, Mrs. Carter."

"Good evening, Antonio. This is Jack's brother, Dean, and my best friend, Melissa. They're staying with us for a few days, so be sure to give them access."

Antonio studied their faces, as if committing them to memory. "You got it. I hope you enjoy your stay." He tipped his head. "Oh, and Mrs. Carter, tell Mr. Carter we miss him on the field and to get better soon."

Forcing a smile, I told him I would pass along his message, but inside I started to crumble. "I hope you're ready for this," I warned Dean as the elevator dinged and we stepped inside.

Dean nodded. "But can I just say that this place is awesome? A doorman? Lights like Disneyland? I can't wait to see what your apartment looks like."

I held back a chuckle; he sounded like an excited kid. "It's ridiculously nice. We're really lucky."

My mind shot back to the day we first toured this apartment. Jack had the rare day off and had found us this place after researching all morning. It was love at first sight for me, what with the granite countertops, stainless steel appliances, enormous master bedroom, and equally huge marble bathroom. The balcony with its view of the city was simply an added perk that called to my photographic side. To put it mildly, I fell in love the moment I walked through the front door.

Jack, on the other hand, didn't even explore the apartment at all. Waiting for my approval, he said all that mattered was that I liked it. He had been sold on the doorman, the twenty-four hour security, and the private gym.

"Cassie? Hellooo." Melissa waved a hand in front of my eyes, forcing me back to reality.

"Sorry," I said with a sheepish smile. "I was just remembering the first time we saw this place." I shook off the memory and stepped out of the elevator.

When I opened the front door, the shadows from the television and the city lights danced across the otherwise darkened walls. Floor-to-ceiling windows provided the most beautiful views of the city, and Melissa gasped as she pulled her suitcase through the entryway.

"Wow. That's stunning. What a view, Cass."

"Holy shit, that's gorgeous," Dean agreed as the wheels on

his suitcase squeaked.

Melissa leaned toward me and whispered, "Where's Jack?"

"I'm trying to sleep, but you're all so fucking loud." Jack's snarky voice sliced through our otherwise enjoyable moment, putting us all on notice.

I pursed my lips together, my eyes instantly filling with tears, and waved a hand in the direction of the couch.

"Aren't you a peach?" Dean mocked, before walking through the living room and flipping on every switch he could find.

The apartment lit up like a showroom and Jack cursed. "Turn those off. Fuck." He glared at his brother in the bright light, and for a moment I was embarrassed at his appearance. He refused to shave and wouldn't let me help him, so his beard was overgrown and he looked really scruffy.

"Stop being a dick," Dean snapped back.

"Stop being here," Jack growled before covering his eyes with a pillow.

"Nice to see you, too." Dean moved away from his brother and walked back toward his things. "Where's the guest room?"

I wiped the lone tear that fell, disheartened to witness this kind of interaction between them. "Sorry. It's over here." I led him to the far left side of the apartment. "Our room is on the other side of the kitchen. This is your bathroom, so make yourself at home."

"I've never seen him like this. He didn't even make eye contact with me," Dean said with a wince.

"Told you it was bad."

"Yeah, I know," he breathed out. "I need a minute."

"Of course. Take all the time you need. It's not like he's going anywhere." I turned to leave the room and ran straight into Melissa.

"Is this our room?" she asked, peering around me.

"Yep. Bathroom's behind you. Make yourself at home." I sucked in a deep breath, then leaned down to give her a hug and whispered, "Take care of Dean, please. Don't fuck with him any more. You're going to break him."

Melissa coughed against me, shocked by my words. "Oh my God, shut up."

"I'm not kidding. He needs you," I said pointedly before walking away.

New York
State of Mind
Jack

The next morning, I woke up with a back sore from sleeping on the couch two nights in a row. The constant barrage of conversation surrounding me reminded me that my brother and Melissa were here.

Great.

It had to be clear to everyone that I was avoiding my wife. My mind was spinning out of control with thoughts I never imagined having. The idea of my baseball career being over wrecked me.

Literally fucking ruined me.

I couldn't function like a normal human being anymore. The thought turned me into an unrecognizable asshole. And the worst part was, I knew it. I was completely aware of my behavior, but it was like I couldn't stop it. My head would tell my mouth not to say what it was about to say, but my mouth would say it anyway.

And even though I wanted to take it all back, I didn't. It's as if I started digging a hole and once I got in it, I couldn't stop digging. I wanted to get low enough so that I could bury myself inside and never see the light of day again. That was what losing baseball felt like.

"Hey, asshole," my little brother's voice called out and I cleared my throat.

"What do you want, dick?"

"I want to sightsee and you're taking me," he demanded.

I almost fucking laughed. There was no way I was going to let Dean boss me around. "I'm sure Cassie would be better at that sort of thing." Even that sentence came out sounding like a slam against her.

"I'm sure she would be too. But I want you to take me. You need to get out of this house. And you look like shit."

Melissa laughed and I shot her an evil look. "Shut up, Fun-Size. Why are you even here?"

"Fuck you, Jack. I'm here because you're being an asshole to my best friend. And someone has to give a shit about her."

Her words stung, but I pretended not to be fazed. Each breath I sucked in pierced my heart more deeply. I had to stop hurting Cassie, but I couldn't. Why couldn't I just fucking stop? Pushing up from the couch, I glared at the three of them sitting at the table, then growled at Dean, "Be ready to leave in ten."

"So, where we going?" my brother asked after we left the girls at the apartment, his face filled with excitement.

"You like it here, don't you?" I teased, my mood already lifting. The trees were losing their leaves and the weather was changing. That was definitely one of the coolest things about living here—the feeling in the air as the seasons changed.

He looked around. "I've never seen anyplace like it."

And he was right. There was nothing like this in Southern California, and New York did have a magical feel to it. That is, once you looked past all the dirt, trash, and large rats running around. Hell, even that shit didn't bother me.

"Well, I haven't seen much, to be honest," I admitted. "I don't have much time to play tourist, but you've got to see Central Park. It's huge." I punched my brother in the arm.

"How far is it? Do we drive there? Or walk? Or take the subway?"

I shook my head. "Shut the fuck up. Jesus, you're like a damn chick. We'll walk there. It's nice out and that way you can see more. You can't see shit if we're underground in the train."

Dean agreed and basically walked with his head up his ass, staring up and around the whole time. "Dude, you need to be aware of your surroundings. At least act like you're paying attention or someone's going to mug you," I said, shaking my head.

"What?" He shot me an incredulous glance.

"It's a big fucking city. Shit happens. Don't act stupid."

A group of young couples passed by us and I pulled my hat lower, trying to avoid being noticed. "I think that was Jack Carter! Oh my God," a girl squawked from behind me.

"Shit," I mumbled to no one in particular.

"That is him," I heard another one say. "Look, he has a cast on and everything. Jack? Excuse me, Jack?" The sound of shoes slamming against the pavement stopped me.

I turned to face the group of twenty-somethings.

"Can we have your autograph?" one of the girls asked hopefully.

Lifting up my broken arm, I shrugged. "Can't really sign anything with a broken hand, sorry."

"Oh yeah, stupid me." The girl smacked her forehead. "Can we get a picture with you, then?"

I sucked in a breath and glanced around before agreeing. "Sure."

After one shot, I'd hoped we were done, but everyone had their own camera phone, and wanted their own picture. Soon a small crowd had formed, all clamoring for the same thing. Trying to keep my irritation in check, I obliged everyone wanting a photo with me before turning toward my brother, who had willingly turned photographer. "Sorry. Maybe we should have taken the train," I said before continuing up East Fifty-Ninth.

"Nah. It's cool," he said with a smile. "Plus, you were actually nice to them."

"Fuck off."

"See? What's your problem, man?"

"Don't start with me," I said through clenched teeth. I didn't want to talk about this. My thoughts alone caused me enough grief. The last thing I wanted to do was actually talk about them.

"I will start with you," Dean said harshly. "You're being a real dick. And to Cassie, of all people. Do you want her to fucking leave you?"

I stopped walking. Mid. Fucking. Step.

"What the hell did you just say to me?" I glared at my little brother, my heart fucking pounding out each beat against my chest.

Dean hardened his expression. "She won't put up with this forever. Eventually she'll leave you. And it will be your own fault."

I moved to shove him but he dodged me. "Don't say that. Don't you dare fucking say that."

"What? You don't want to hear the truth? You're unbearable right now. I've never seen you like this. And heaven forbid your hand not heal right and—"

I cut him off, not wanting to hear the next fucking word that came out of his mouth. Right now all I wanted to do was punch him in it. "Shut up, Dean. Shut the fuck up right now. You don't know what it's like. You have no idea how I feel."

"Then tell me! Tell someone!" he shouted and I swore the entire city stopped moving so they could listen.

"Keep your goddamned voice down," I demanded and resumed walking. His fingers wrapped around the sleeve of my shirt and he pulled me back. "What the hell?"

"We're talking about this," he said as he leveled his gaze to mine. "So figure out someplace we can go to do it. I'm not taking no for an answer."

My stubborn nature refused to let me respond. Instead I marched forward, heading in the direction of the park. Central Park was massive. There were plenty of places we could go to talk and not be surrounded by prying ears.

As we crossed over Fifth Avenue, I turned to Dean and pointed. "That's the Plaza Hotel. It's Cassie's favorite, she's absolutely in love with it. And that fountain."

Dean looked in the direction of the hotel. "I can see why. It's fantastic."

"Come on. The park's right there."

I could tell Dean still didn't get it. He didn't know how grand this park was. I'm sure he assumed that the park would be the size of one of our parks at home. I should have told him that Central Park was more like Griffith Park, only more awesome.

Entering through the southeast corner of the park, it didn't take long until the sounds of the outside world started to fade. The park was alluring in that way. You could cross the street in front of screaming cabs and tourists, and before you knew it you'd entered a world where birds were chirping, people were jogging, and the only other sound you heard were those of horseshoes clacking against the pavement. Submersed inside this world, it was easy to forget anything existed outside of it.

A few more steps and we were at the pond. "Wow," Dean said with a smile. "So this is Central Park, huh?"

I laughed. Shit. I hadn't laughed in days and my face knew it. It hurt. "This is barely Central Park."

"What do you mean?"

"Dude, this is the pond. There's a lake, a merry-go-round,

an ice skating rink, baseball fields, a zoo, the meadow where they have concerts and shit. This place is huge. I still haven't seen the whole thing."

"That doesn't sound like a park. That sounds like a city."

I shrugged. "It sorta is, like a city within a city." Spotting some large boulders in the distance, I sped toward them as Dean followed behind. I climbed up on the largest one and sat on top. Dean climbed up next to me.

"Does it hurt?" he asked.

"Does what hurt?"

"Your hand. I see you tucking it against you every now and then, and I wondered if it hurts."

I looked down at the cast covering my pitching arm. "Do I really do that? I didn't notice."

"That's not an answer," he said.

I hadn't admitted it to anyone. Not even to the team's doctor, but yes, my hand hurt. It fucking killed me. As far as they knew, I was taking their prescribed painkillers. But the truth was that I wasn't.

"Yeah, it hurts," I admitted.

"How bad?"

"It's a constant pain. I can feel my heart beating in my fingertips. It fucking kills me."

Dean's head tipped to one side as though he were confused, or worried. "That can't be good. They gave you painkillers, right?"

I nodded sharply.

"They're not working, then? You have to tell them."

I huffed out a breath. "I'm not taking them."

"What? Why on earth not?" His face scrunched up with confusion and I looked around at the green trees surrounding us.

"Because I don't do that shit. I don't do drugs. I've never taken a painkiller in my life and I've heard they're addictive. What if I get addicted to them?"

Dean laughed. Full-out belly laughed, and I resisted punching him in the gut to shut him up.

"You're not going to get addicted," he said. "Just cut them in half. Whenever you start to feel the pain, take half of whatever they prescribed you. Soon, the pain will stop and you won't need them. You're not Superman, Jack."

"Says you."

"I say that because I know you, brother," he insisted.

"And I say no because I've seen way too many guys get addicted to shit. I refuse to be one of them."

He sighed, clearly more convinced of my own strength than I was. "Here." He pulled an envelope from his back pocket and tossed it onto my lap.

"What the hell is this?"

"It's a letter from Gran."

"You read it?" I asked, my tone defensive.

He frowned at me and snapped, "Does it look like I read it?"

I turned the envelope around, and ripped open the seal.

Dear Jack,

Sometimes life doesn't unfold the way we want it to. You, of all people, have learned that lesson all too well. First with your parents, then with Cassie and that other horrible girl, and now with baseball.

Gramps and I are so sorry that your hand is broken. And we know how much you must be hurting because of it. But, Jack, I'm hearing things about your behavior and attitude toward your wife that I cannot condone. I did not raise you to be mean, rude, or disrespectful to the one person who has loved you at your worst.

I know you feel as though your life IS baseball, but the reality is your life is so much more than just your chosen profession. True, baseball is a part of your life, but it is only a part. No matter how wholeheartedly you think differently, you are not baseball, and baseball is not you. It will not last forever. Nothing does, dear. Nothing except love, of course.

Eventually your hand will heal, but if you ruin things with your wife, I fear your heart never will. Remember how it felt to lose her. And don't let it happen again.

Remember who you are. You're Jack Carter, the boy with the unbreakable spirit and resolve. The boy who doesn't take no for an answer when it's something he wants. You've been like that since you were five years old. And I know you haven't changed. So stop throwing this little pity party of yours and get your priorities straight.

You know how I feel about flying, so DO NOT MAKE ME GET ON A PLANE AND FLY OUT THERE! I will if you leave me no choice, but I won't be happy about it. The next time I talk to that wife of yours, she'd better not be crying.

I love you,

Gran (Gramps too)

"Fuck," I breathed out, running my free hand through my hair. "Cassie cried to Gran?"

"What?" Dean asked, clearly as clueless as I was. I handed him the letter so he could read it himself and sucked in a long, slow breath. They were right. Everyone was. I was being a fucking asshole to the one person who deserved it the least.

Cassie.

Shit.

My beautiful Kitten. My heart. My soul. The only thing in this world I loved more than baseball. Had I somehow forgotten that? I certainly acted like it. I owed her a million apologies, and a thousand explanations. And I hoped that they would be enough.

All I'd done since I met this girl was bring her grief. It wasn't enough to have some good times when you overshadowed them with bad ones. I needed to stop being such a dick and get my head on straight.

"Remind me to never upset her, okay? I don't think I could handle a Gran letter like this." Dean's eyes were wide as he handed the letter back to me.

I grabbed it and folded it carefully, then tucked it into my jeans pocket.

"We have to get out of here. I need to go home." I rose from the rock and climbed back down it, trying not to fall on my ass and break my other hand.

I thought Dean might be disappointed, but he sat there looking at me with a shit-eating grin plastered all over his face. "Thank God!" he called out toward the sky.

"Now we're religious?"

"If that's what it takes, then hell yeah, I'm religious." He hopped down and patted my back. "Let's get you home to your wife."

I hailed a cab the second my foot hit the crowded sidewalk outside the park. We scooted into the backseat and I gave the cabbie our address.

"So, do you want to talk about it?" Dean looked at me and the sympathy in his eyes made me cringe.

"I do," I said with a nod. "But not with you."

"Uh, thanks."

I laughed. "I didn't mean it like that. I just need to talk to my wife first."

Dean nodded his head in agreement. "Definitely. But then I want to hear about it, okay?"

"Okay. Thanks for coming out here." I punched his thigh playfully, wanting him to know that having him here made me happy.

"I'm your brother. I'd do anything for you," he said, and I knew he meant it.

"Same here." Of course I didn't need to say it, but I wanted to.

I'd missed Dean more than I realized. It was easy to forget how much you miss people when you didn't see them every day. I must be more of the *out of sight, out of mind* type. Unless we were talking about Kitten; then all bets were off. Because when it came to her, I was more the *distance makes the heart grow fonder* type. Or you could just call me *pussy* for short.

I burst through our front door with Dean on my heels, praying Cassie would be home. When I found her in the kitchen table with Melissa, her green eyes instantly found mine before they looked away, the pain I'd caused her abundantly clear.

Fuck.

She hated me. I'd hate me too. How many times had I said that before?

Ignoring Melissa, I rushed to Cassie, grabbed her hand in my good one, and pulled her into our bedroom, slamming the door behind us. Without a word, I pulled her over to the bed and sat down, pulling her to a seat on the mattress next to me.

"Jack, what are you—"

"Shhh. Please. Just wait here for a minute," I begged. Leaning over and placing my head against my cast, I closed my eyes and silently berated myself. Cassie didn't move and I didn't either, afraid that if I disturbed the emotional dust settling around us, I'd mess it all up again.

I sat there a good ten minutes without moving a muscle. When I finally sat up and opened my eyes, tears began to spill down my cheeks.

"Oh God, Kitten. I'm sorry, I'm so sorry. Please, please don't leave me."

"Leave you?" Her eyebrows flew up and her eyes grew wide, as if she had no idea what I was talking about.

"I fucked up. I'm just so scared for what all this means, you know?" I held my cast-covered arm in the air and she nodded. "I'm not ready to lose baseball. I'm not ready for my career to be over. And I've taken it all out on you."

She started to cry. No words came, just tears, so I went on. "I know you probably hate me. Or you're mad at me. And I deserve it. But please know how sorry I am. I'll never treat you like this again, I promise."

"Don't make promises you can't keep," she said, her voice barely above a whisper.

I shifted over, closing the space between us, and pulled her body against mine. "I'll never treat you like this again," I said against her hair as she trembled in my arms. "I am so sorry for the way I've been acting. I'm scared. Terrified I'll never be able to throw again. I'm not ready. I'm not ready to lose baseball. But I'll never be ready to lose you."

Cassie pulled back slightly so she could look up at me. "Jack," she said softly as I wiped the tears from her face. "Why are you so convinced your career's over?"

I paused, my mind instantly thinking about my parents both choosing to abandon me and Dean at different times. The helpless feeling started to sweep over me again, filling me with dread. It amazed me how after all these years, one simple past action could send me into a tailspin. "I don't know. Because I love baseball so much and I want it so badly, I'm afraid it will be taken from me. Like I don't deserve to have the things that I love."

"You have me," she said softly as she pinned me with her gaze.

"But I lost you. I had to get you back. Nothing comes easy. I fuck things up. I'm sure it's only a matter of time before I fuck up baseball too."

Her face scrunched up and she shouted, "Stop it!" which surprised me. "Just stop it. I hate this side of you. It's like you're quitting and that's <u>not</u> the Jack I know. Stop being so complacent. Be a fucking man. Be the man I know and love."

I nodded, her words striking me square in the chest. I wanted to yell at her for being so harsh, but she was right and I needed to hear it. "You're right. I'm filled with self-pity and it's a joke. That's why I don't give a fuck if baseball tries to quit on me, I'm not going to let it."

The corners of her mouth started to tilt upward with my confession. "That's what I like to hear."

"Baby, I am really sorry. I can never take back the way I acted, but I can promise you I'll never do it again." I fell to my knees. "I know all I do is apologize to you for fucking up, but please, Kitten. I need you by my side. I'll always need you by my side. Say you forgive me. Please."

I waited. Waited for her to say she forgave me. Waited for her to say she loved me and she'd never leave me. I'd wait forever to hear those words if she wanted me to. She lowered herself to the floor next to me and took my face in the palm of her hands. God, her hands were soft.

Her green eyes stared through me, intense and ferocious as she spoke. "I'm your wife. I vowed in front of our friends and family that I would love you until I died. And I plan on doing just that, but please," she paused, "stop making it so hard for me." Her lips found mine and my chest instantly eased with relief.

"I love you. I fucking love you." My tongue explored the inside of her mouth and I wanted to bury myself in her. "I need you. Now."

"Jack, we have guests."

"They aren't guests. They can wait. I need to be inside you. You're my home. I need to be home right now."

Cassie hesitated and pulled away slightly. "Don't do it like last time." She looked down as I struggled to remember what she was talking about.

Then I remembered. I was rough with her the night I got hurt, and that was the last time we'd been together. "Oh shit, Cassie. Did I hurt you?" Her head shook slowly back and forth, her eyes still focused on the floor. "I did, didn't I? I fucking hurt you, didn't I?"

"You didn't *hurt* me," she said slowly.

"Then what? What did I do? I know I was rough and I'm sorry. I'll never forgive myself if you're not okay." I couldn't believe this. It was one fuck-up after another with me. How could I be so stupid all the time?

She looked up, her eyes meeting mine. "You scared me a little. Not a lot. But still."

I leaned my head into my hand and wiped at my eyes. "I'm so sorry. Kitten, please. I needed to feel like a man because I felt so useless on the ball field. I wanted to dominate something, but I didn't even think about how it would make you feel. I just wanted to make myself feel better. 'Cause I'm a selfish prick."

"I just need a little time, okay? I love you and we'll be fine, but I need us to go slow right now," she suggested and my dick ached.

"Absolutely. We'll go at your pace. Whatever you want. I'll do whatever you want." I pulled her against me and hugged her tight. She probably couldn't breathe, but I needed her to be that close to me.

"Thank you. We should probably get out there." She smiled and I pushed up from the floor before reaching for her.

"I really am sorry," I whispered against her ear before hugging her again.

"I know. Just talk to me, please. You can't get like that. I can't get like that. It doesn't work for us when we don't talk."

"I've never dealt with this before," I admitted and she nodded against my chest.

"I know. But we'll deal with it together. We're a team, remember? You told me that. It's you and me against the world, Carter."

"For fucking ever," I said before covering her mouth with mine and pouring all my love for her into that kiss. She moaned and her body relaxed against me. We'd be okay. We just needed a little time.

When we finally left our bedroom, Melissa and Dean were sitting on the couch watching some chick flick. He had his arm around her and she was leaning against him.

"Figures you'd grow a vagina the second I leave you alone," I teased and Dean breathed out a sigh. "What the hell are you two watching?"

Dean shoved a fist in the air. "My brother's back!"

"Are you done being an asshole, Asshole?" Melissa chirped in my direction.

"Are you done being a cock tease to my brother, Cock-Tease?" I chirped back.

Cassie's hand landed hard against my chest. "Jack! Leave them alone."

"I was planning on it, until you shot me down." I threw her a glance and flashed a smile in her direction.

"Crash and burn, huh, big brother?" Dean asked.

"I wouldn't talk if I were you," I warned.

Cassie cleared her throat. "Enough with the dick measuring. Jeez."

Melissa turned her head around. "Oh my God, go put a shirt on," she shouted at my ripped chest. "Wait! Get over here."

I knew she wanted me.

I sauntered over to where they were lying on the couch and she reached for my pecs. "Hey, keep your hands off the goods, lady," I teased.

"You wish." Melissa rolled her eyes and grabbed at my

necklace. "She gave you her key?"

I sucked in a breath and pulled the key from her grip. "Yeah. The night I got hurt."

"Pretty cool," she said with a smile.

Cassie closed a drawer and yelled out, "Can we order dinner in? I'm starving. Unless you guys wanna go out? I'm sorta spent, to be honest, but I could rally."

That was my girl, always putting everyone else's wants and needs above her own. I knew she was exhausted after everything we'd been through, but she'd still go get all dolled up and head out for the night if that was what my brother and her best friend wanted to do.

I shot Dean a look that said I'd fucking kill him if he made her go out. Thank God he could read my mind.

"I'd rather stay in," Dean called out while holding my gaze. "We can go out tomorrow. Is that okay with you?" He glanced at Melissa.

"I don't care what we do. I'm comfortable right here." She leaned her tiny body into his and sighed.

He winked at me, then shouted, "Order in!"

Note to self: Remind Dean to never fucking wink at me again.

It's Just Sex

Jack

The next morning I woke up to Cassie sleeping on my chest. My left arm was pressed against her back, which I figured was a complete waste since I couldn't feel her skin through my cast.

She'd initiated sex last night and I let her control the pace. I figured she'd make me wait weeks to earn back her trust in the bedroom, but thankfully she wanted it just as badly as I did. After apologizing with my tongue until she came in my mouth, I entered her slowly, making sure nothing I did would remind her of the other night. It didn't take long for her body to give itself over to me and for her mind to follow. Thank God.

No matter how much hurt and pain we'd caused each other in the past, the fact was that we were in it for the long haul. We trusted each other. Sometimes we lost our way, but we always found our way back. I never wanted that to end. And I never wanted to be the cause of it again. I hated that I scared her. What kind of asshole scares his wife during sex?

I tangled my good fingers through the strands of her long hair, surprised at how soft it always felt. She stirred against me. "Morning, babe," she said against my chest.

"Morning, Kitten."

Her head shot up from my chest, leaving it cold and empty. "Oh my God. Do you remember what we heard last night?" She covered her mouth to stop from laughing too loudly.

I had forgotten. "We don't know what we heard."

"Oh, bullshit! You know as well as I do they were totally having sex in our guest room!"

"Maybe they were just playing Monopoly. With their mouths," I suggested with a smile.

She snorted. "Remind me to ask Melissa how Dean plays Monopoly because it sounded like she was really enjoying it."

"That's 'cause he's a Carter," I said matter-of-factly.

"You guys are good at board games?"

Smartass.

"I'm good at everything. Who knows what Dean's good at." I rolled on top of her, pressing my hard-on against her.

"No way! I need to shower."

"Let me get you dirty first," I whispered against her ear, taking the lobe into my mouth and sucking.

"How about you come clean me off instead?" She wriggled out from under me and the sight of her naked body caused my dick to throb even more.

Shower sex isn't the same when you have a saran-wrapped cast on your good arm. But I powered through it because I'm a team-fucking-player.

When I walked into the living room awhile later, my brother was already at the table eating cereal. Smiling to himself. He looked like a complete asshole.

"Someone get some last night?" I gave his back a hard slap and he turned to smack my arm away, but missed.

"A gentleman doesn't kiss and tell," he responded before spooning another bite of food into this mouth.

"You know," I said as I sat down across from him and poured cereal into my own bowl. "Sound really carries in this place. I never knew that before last night."

He choked on his cereal. "You don't say?"

I handed him a napkin. "Oh, I do say. I say very loudly and very scream-like," I teased.

Cassie entered the room and sat down next to me at the table. She gave Dean a sweet smile and asked, "So, how was Monopoly? It sounds like you're a *really* good player."

I fucking lost it. I laughed so hard I almost spit food across the table. When Melissa finally came out of the guest bedroom, I noticed my little brother's smile grow wider. As she neared, his eyes lit up and he reached for her. His fingertips barely grazed her exposed skin before she angled her body away and picked the seat farthest from him. I only noticed all this shit because I was paying attention, not because I'm a pussy or anything.

"Are you serious right now?" Dean asked her, his tone instantly angry.

I sat up straighter, finding myself intrigued. The idea of my brother standing up for himself impressed me.

Melissa's eyes narrowed as her cheeks reddened and she looked away. "Don't do this here, Dean."

"Don't do what? Are you just going to pretend like nothing happened last night?"

I knew it.

Of course I knew it.

"I didn't say that," she said in an indifferent tone.

"So, what then? We'll just go back to being 'friends,' or whatever the fuck we are?"

Cassie cleared her throat and I gave my brother a swift kick under the table. He glared at me, his cool facade slowly unraveling. Melissa stayed quiet, avoiding any eye contact as Dean looked back and forth between her face and mine.

He shoved out of his chair, almost tossing it into the wall before grabbing his cereal bowl and throwing it a little too roughly into the sink. The sound of it breaking echoed throughout the apartment and his eyes grew wide. "Shit. I'm sorry, Cass."

I looked down at my cereal and shook my head. Little brother couldn't even be mean when he was mad.

"It's okay. Don't worry about it. It's only a dish," she said, walking away from the table and over toward him.

Dean lowered his chin and stared at the floor as Cassie wrapped her arms around him and squeezed. He hugged her back for a second before pushing her away and jumping to his feet. "I need to get the fuck out of here."

"Hey!" I shouted and Dean stopped midstep. "Don't

fucking push my wife like that. I will hit you, I don't care who you are."

My temper flared as he stalked into the guest room and slammed the door. Right on his heels, I knocked hard on the door, causing the knuckles on my good hand to ache immediately. "Dean?" I shouted and turned the knob without waiting for a response.

I stuck my head inside the room and when my gaze met his, I could see in Dean's eyes that he was falling apart. "I'm taking you out." It wasn't a question.

"Yeah. You are."

My brother's response made me laugh. "I'll call Matteo. He's coming too. We need a guys' day."

"We're best friends with the guy who kissed your wife now?" Dean's sour comment caused me to sharply inhale.

"Don't be a dick. He still works for us, doesn't he? If I didn't trust him, he wouldn't be anywhere near Cassie. Plus, he's married and has a baby on the way. And he knows my forgiveness was a one-time deal. He tries any of that shit again and I'll fucking kill him."

Walking into the kitchen, I pulled Cassie aside and kissed her sweet lips. "Kitten, I'm going to take Dean out. Talk to your friend. Find out what the fuck her deal is. This shit between them needs to stop."

"No joke. I feel so bad for your brother. I'll talk to her. Or at least, I'll try."

"I love you." I kissed her cheek.

"Love you too." She smiled and I wanted to kick myself for ever being mean to her.

My cell phone beeped soon afterward, letting me know that Matteo was waiting downstairs. I shouted to Dean, "Let's go. Matteo's waiting."

Dean appeared and I ushered him out the door without another word. Once in the lobby, I pointed Matteo out to him.

"Jesus, Jack. That's the guy you hired to drive Cassie around the city? What the hell's wrong with you?"

Jack shrugged. "What can I say? I'm overly confident and cocky. Have we met?"

We walked through the revolving door and Matteo extended his hand. "Hi, Dean. It's nice to meet you."

"It's nice to meet you too. I've heard a lot about you," Dean added, his tone wary.

Matteo opened the door and walked toward the driver's side and hopped in. "I'm sure you have," he said as he caught Dean's gaze in the rearview mirror. "I'll apologize to you as well, if you'd like."

"Nah. She wasn't my girlfriend." Dean looked at me. "You're lucky Cassie didn't leave you for him. Hell, I'm about to leave you for him. Are you looking for a new brother? Want to adopt me?" Dean blurted out.

Matteo laughed from the front seat. "You bet, kid. 'Cause us Italian New Yorkers don't have enough family members."

"What about your wife? Does she have any sisters?"

I sat up straighter. "Holy shit, does she? I never even thought about that. I mean, of course, I wouldn't but—" I stopped abruptly, realizing that didn't exactly come out right.

Matteo chuckled and shook his head. "Sorry. She's all mine and there's only one of her."

"Fucking figures," Dean muttered under his breath.

"Do you care where we drink?" Matteo asked.

"Somewhere private. No sports bars or shit like that," I insisted.

"Do you really think I'd take you to a sports bar? I'm hurt, man. Crushed."

"So, where are we going?" Dean asked as the car slowed to a stop.

I looked out the window, recognizing the entrance from a profile shoot Cassie had done on historical bars in the city.

"I know this place. Cassie photographed it for the magazine."

Matteo threw his head back. "That's right! I remember that. This place used to be a speakeasy. Sinatra used to hang out here with his boys. It's pretty cool. Lots of history."

We walked into the dimly lit bar and paused for a second so our eyes could adjust. Coming inside from the bright afternoon sunshine, this place seemed almost as dark as night. Giving the bartender a nod, Matteo pointed toward the back of the room, where a velvet rope hung. The three of us headed toward the small table behind the rope. The place was virtually empty, except for the few guys sitting at the bar. I prayed they wouldn't recognize me.

"I'll grab us drinks," Matteo offered. "What are we having?"

"Beer for me. Whatever's on tap and good," I responded.

"Same here," Dean added.

I waited for Matteo to return before I started asking Dean any questions, figuring he might have some outside perspective to offer. A few minutes later he came back, balancing all three beers in his hands before setting them on the table without spilling a drop.

"You're a fucking boss," I said, complimenting him on his skills before tapping my glass against his.

"Ah, I used to tend bar in college," he said, and I laughed, almost spitting my beer at him.

"Why am I not surprised?" I took a deep swig of the beer, closing my eyes for a second in appreciation of its icy goodness.

"The real question is why is that so funny?"

I shrugged and said, "I have no fucking idea." Then I laughed some more, convinced my body and mind were out to betray me after I'd treated them so badly this past week.

Dean looked back and forth between me and Matteo. "I don't get why you're laughing? What the fuck did I miss?"

"I have no idea," Matteo said with a raised eyebrow as I pulled myself together.

Why the fuck was I suddenly giggling like a fourteen-year-old schoolgirl? It was like once I started laughing, I couldn't fucking stop. And knowing that I needed the release only made it worse. I focused on my breathing, pretending I was on the mound during a crisis. I needed to calm down.

My breathing slowed and I looked at my baby brother. "So, what happened?"

"Are you done with your giggle fit?" Dean asked, apparently full of piss and vinegar.

"For now. So, tell me what happened," I urged before taking a swig of my ice cold beer. I loved cold beer.

Dean sighed and rolled his beer between his palms. "We

had sex last night and I thought that changed things between us."

"Wait, why would that change things? This wasn't the first time you two …" I paused, eyeing him.

"Yes. It was the first time. Melissa knows how I feel about her. She knows." He shook his head and I could see that he was hurting.

"Maybe it wasn't good sex," I said with a laugh to lighten the mood.

"Fuck you," Dean shot back. "It was the hottest sex I've ever had in my life."

I leaned toward him. "For you, maybe. But what about her?"

He narrowed his eyes. "The whole thing was hot. She practically begged for it, more than once. I think she liked it."

I shrugged. "Then I don't know what to tell you. That girl's always been a pain in the ass to figure out. Even Kitten's no help."

"What do you mean?" Matteo sipped his beer and waited for my response. I'd filled him in a little bit in the past about Dean and Melissa's history, but he didn't know much. Hell, none of us really did.

"I asked her once what Melissa's problem was and she said she didn't know. That she's always hooked up with guys and shit, but she never really likes them."

"That doesn't make any sense. Who's like that?" Dean spat, his temper finally showing up for the party.

I lifted my beer. "Me."

"Great," he said with a snort. "So she's a female version of you?"

I shrugged. "I'm just saying. It's sort of a guy's way of thinking, if you break it down. And that probably works for you since you're such a chick."

"Really?" he snarled at me.

Shaking my head, I grinned. "I'm only fucking around, little brother."

The scantily clad bartender walked over to our table and the three of us immediately shut up. She asked if she could get us anything and I ordered three shots of tequila. Once she walked away, I looked at Matteo's worried expression and shrugged. "It seemed like a good idea at the time."

"If I drink too much, we'll need a driver for the driver," he explained and I laughed.

"Where were we?" I paused and looked at Dean. "Oh yeah. You're a chick and Melissa's a dude."

"It's not funny. And I'm over it. I'm done. And when we get back to your place, I'm telling her that." He sounded determined and angry, and it hit me that those feelings were exactly what he needed. My brother needed to take control of his dick back.

"Good," I told him.

"Yeah?" Dean eyed me, then downed the last of his beer.

I loved Melissa because she was my wife's best friend, and because she'd been there for me on more than one occasion. But she'd been stringing my brother along since I've known her. So yeah, I supported my brother's decision to tell her to shit or get off the pot.

"You deserve the best and if she's not going to be that, then fuck her. It's not like you haven't given her enough chances to make a decision already. No girl's worth all this hassle. Except mine. But she'd never pull this kind of shit."

"And mine," Matteo added.

"Trina is a good one, bro." I raised my glass toward him before taking a drink.

"Yeah, yeah. I already know how fucking great both your wives are. Can we get back to me?"

"We never left," Matteo reassured him.

"So, what do you think? You don't really know either of us. What's your take?" Dean lifted his chin in Matteo's direction. "You know, as an outsider?"

Matteo looked between me and my brother before saying, "I don't know the whole story between you two, but it sounds like she's just leading you on. She knows how you feel about her, right?"

"Absolutely," Dean answered.

"Without a doubt? You've told her?" Matteo asked.

Dean's face scrunched up. "Yes. More than once."

The bartender appeared and placed our shots on the table. I handed her my credit card and told her to bring us the check, wanting her to leave as soon as possible so we could get to the bottom of this shit with my brother.

"Okay, so what does she say?" Matteo asked, getting us back on track.

"She usually avoids it. But she'll kiss me to shut me up or say she likes me too, but—"

"But what?" I interrupted.

"She likes me too, but she doesn't want a boyfriend right

now. Or she can't. Or some other bullshit excuse. I don't know. It's all lies. Fuck her. I'm done."

"I think that's exactly what she needs." Matteo stared at my brother and a light bulb went off inside my head.

"Matteo's right. You have to make sure she knows you're done."

"I just said that I would."

I slapped my hand against his shoulder. "But you have to follow through. She needs to lose you to figure out once and for all what the fuck she wants."

"This isn't a game to me, Jack. I'm done. She just wrecked me and I won't let her do it anymore. She either wants to be with me or she doesn't. Either way, I'm fucking done waiting around for her to make up her mind." I watched as he downed his shot.

"Ready to go back home?" I asked.

"You bet."

The three of us rose to our feet as Matteo pushed his tequila shot toward Dean and he downed it as well. I signed off on our tab with the bartender before we headed out of the darkness and into the bright Manhattan sunlight.

"I need to park the car. Apparently my wife is upstairs with yours," Matteo said from the driver's seat. "Do you want me to drop you two off at the entrance and then meet you inside?"

"Don't be an asshole. We'll park the car and go in

together."

Dean stayed quiet the elevator ride up to the twenty-third floor and he was the first one off when it came to a stop. I'd never seen him so fired up before. Matteo and I jogged to keep up with him, neither one of us wanting to miss a minute of this show. It was a shitty move, I know, but the idea of seeing my super sweet brother be a dick to someone was fucking exciting.

He walked through the door before any of us and grabbed Melissa by the arm. "We need to talk. Now."

"Ouch. Jeez, Dean, let me go."

"No. You want to talk in private or do you want me to say what I have to say right here in front of all these people?" He waved his arm in our direction and I looked at Cassie, who was currently glaring at me.

I mouthed "not my fault" to her and she narrowed her eyes at me.

Melissa glanced around the room at Trina, Cassie, Matteo, and me before whispering, "In private," and stalked off behind Dean's giant frame.

"Hey, Trina!" I smiled at Matteo's wife. "You look great."

"Stop hitting on my wife," Matteo joked.

"You don't want to go there, do you? We can if you want," I joked back.

Dean's shouting stopped our conversation as all four of us turned our heads in the direction of the guest bedroom. We were mesmerized by the sound of Dean actually yelling at someone. And knowing that *the someone* was Fun-Size. The whole thing seemed insane.

Despite the closed bedroom door, we could hear absolutely

everything. It was awesome.

"You acted like it didn't matter. Like nothing between us ever fucking matters. Why? Why do you do that?" he yelled, the frustration in his voice coming through loud and clear from a room away.

"I don't know," she answered softly.

"Bullshit! That's bullshit! You do know. Do you have any idea how much of an idiot I felt like this morning when you walked out of the room? I thought things were different after last night, but I was wrong. I'm always fucking wrong when it comes to you."

"Why are you so mad?" Her voice was shaking, and knowing girls, I knew tears couldn't be far behind.

"Are you joking? You make me feel like a fucking fool over and over again and I'm sick of it. I'm not doing it anymore. I'm done with this." His voice was cold and I glanced at Cassie, who looked like she was holding her breath.

"What do you mean, you're 'done with this'?"

"With this. With you. I'm not doing this anymore."

"So, that's it? We're not even friends?" she asked, her voice rising in pitch.

"I don't want to be your friend! How many times do I have to tell you that?" he shouted, and it sounded like he punched something, but I couldn't imagine what. "Damn it, Melissa. I don't want to be your fucking friend, okay? Stop acting like you don't know this already. You know how I feel. And I can't be around you with all this back-and-forth bullshit that you do to me. I've wanted you for two years. Two years!" he yelled and I almost felt bad for eavesdropping. Almost.

"Well, who asked you to want me? I didn't, did I?"

My eyes widened at her response and I shifted closer to Cassie and grabbed her hand. She squeezed it hard.

Dean whistled a sound before responding to her. "No, you sure didn't. Well, you don't have to worry about me anymore. You can delete my phone number from your cell since I won't answer if you call."

The guest bedroom door flew open and none of us even pretended to be doing anything else. We all stared at my little brother as he walked into the kitchen and grabbed a beer from the refrigerator.

I cleared my throat, determined to be a good host. "Dean, this is Trina, Matteo's wife. Trina, this is my little brother, Dean."

Dean smiled, then sauntered over to Trina and shook her hand. "It's nice to meet you, I've heard wonderful things. Sorry about all the yelling."

"It's okay. I understand," she said with a sympathetic smile.

"I love your accent. No one told me you were British," Dean said, laying on the charm.

"And no one told me you were so cute," she flirted back and I had to bite my lip to keep myself from laughing. My brother could use the attention.

Melissa rounded the corner, and Cassie immediately dropped my hand and headed toward her. They disappeared and I heard a door close. I glanced at Matteo and Trina and apologized.

"It's okay. We need to get going anyway. We have reservations in a little bit. It was nice to see you, Jack. And nice to meet you, Dean." Trina kissed my cheek and gave Dean a squeeze and told him, "Personally, I think she's crazy to not be head over heels for you. But don't worry, you'll find the right girl. You're a catch. Don't ever forget that."

"Thanks, Trina. It was nice meeting you. You too, Matteo," Dean said with a nod in his direction. "Thanks for this afternoon."

"That's what adoptive brothers do for each other," he said with a laugh.

I shook Matteo's hand and closed the front door behind them as they left. "How are you feeling?"

My brother peered around the kitchen column to look at me. "I'm still pissed, but I feel good."

"Good. You're right, you know," I offered in consolation.

"About what?"

"Everything you said to her. So don't feel bad when you wake up tomorrow and want to take it all back."

He half smiled. "That's not going to happen."

Slow Recovery

Cassie

I couldn't believe the drama that happened during Dean and Melissa's visit. Hell, I'd only suggested they come out here together because I wanted them to finally get together. I guess that backfired. And now Dean was hurting and I didn't know what Melissa was feeling, but I somehow feel responsible for it all.

Dean refused to sleep in the guest room last night, so he stayed on the couch. I tried to get him to stay in our room with Jack and I'd sleep with Melissa, but he wouldn't budge.

"Just go stay in our bed. It's no big deal, Dean. I'll go stay with Melissa," I offered.

"No, thanks. I like couches," he said with a wink as his gaze looked past me to something over my shoulder.

I turned around and noticed Jack standing behind me. "What were you doing?" I asked him.

"Me? Nothing? Just staring at your ass," Jack said and I laughed.

"Liar!" I smacked my palm against his chest.

"I just told Dean that if he said yes to sleeping in a bed with me that I'd smother him with a pillow and throw his dead body off our balcony. I'm not fucking sleeping with my brother, Kitten, when I can sleep with you."

I tapped my foot against the tile flooring. "You said all that from behind me?"

"Not with words. But the message was conveyed." He ran his finger across his neck like a sinister throat-slasher.

"Dean, I just want you to be comfortable on your last night here. Please let me know if I can do anything for you."

"I'm fine, Sis. Really. Stop worrying."

It was only after his insistence that I finally left him alone and went to bed with Jack. Melissa had fallen asleep pretty soon after our post-fight chat, and both times that I checked on her, she hadn't moved.

She confessed to being rattled by Dean's explosion of emotions and she cried on my shoulder. A lot. But she wouldn't really admit to anything. I kept asking if she liked Dean and she would nod her head, but she wouldn't say much else. Honestly, I was still just as confused now as I was six months ago. Something was preventing Melissa from letting go and loving Dean, but I had no clue what it was. And she wouldn't tell me.

The next morning we all got ready in silence. I insisted that Jack come to the airport with me because I didn't want to deal with the two of them by myself. I had no idea how things would go and I needed all the support I could get. Plus, Jack would be able to tell them to go fuck themselves when all I'd want to do is superglue their body parts together.

Forever.

Dean avoided Melissa entirely. He refused to look in her direction, sit near her, or even acknowledge her existence. One look at her and I could tell it was eating her up inside. She looked like she was breaking. When we got to the airport, the four of us walked together toward the check-in counter. Jack stopped for a couple of pictures, reminding his fans that he couldn't sign anything with his broken hand, as the three of us took care of getting them checked in.

"Dean," Melissa whispered in his direction, but I heard.

"What?" he responded without turning or moving toward her.

"Can we talk?"

"Nope." He turned his head and met her gaze straight on, and my heart cracked in that instant for them both. I hated what they were going through and longed to take their pain away.

"You seriously won't talk to me right now?" Melissa asked, her voice small.

"No, I seriously won't talk to you right now."

The lady at the ticket counter shouted, "Next," and Dean walked up alone. I squeezed my tiny best friend and pulled her head against me. "Thanks for coming out. I really do miss you."

"I miss you too. I hate that you're so far away," she complained.

"I know. Me too. You need to fix this thing with Dean," I suggested and she sighed.

After getting her bags checked, we met the Carter boys in

front of the security line. I hugged Dean tightly. "I love you. I'm going to miss you. Thank you so much for coming out. Come out more, okay? We miss you."

He gave me a big smile. "I will. I'll miss you guys too."

"Tell Gran and Gramps hi for me please!" I added before I forgot. I missed them all the time. I'd never had a couple who were as wise about life as the two of them. They knew what truly mattered in life and they never hesitated to make it known. I had so much to thank them for.

Jack squeezed his younger brother and patted his back so hard it sounded like he broke him. Dean turned toward Melissa and said, "Enjoy your flight."

"What does that mean? Aren't we on the same one?" She looked at me, uncertainty written all over face.

"Not anymore."

Her mouth dropped completely open and mine followed. "Seriously?" she asked.

"Seriously," he deadpanned.

"What flight are you on?"

"Not yours, so don't worry about it." Dean entered the security line and I stood there completely stunned.

"Holy shit," I said to no one in particular.

Melissa's eyes teared up, but she sniffed them back as I gave her one last hug. "I'll call you later." She sucked in a breath and entered the line by herself, now separated from Dean by numerous people.

"Are you going to be okay?" I asked, the shock still overwhelming my senses.

She forced a smile. "Yep."

I reached for my husband's hand and squeezed it hard. Jack told Melissa good-bye again and pulled me toward the exit doors. "I cannot believe he did that," I said, stealing a look into Jack's chocolate-brown eyes.

Jack shot a sideways glance my way. "Hate to admit it, but that was pretty badass."

I sucked in a sharp breath.

"Sorry, Kitten, but she deserves it."

Oh, how I wanted to disagree. I wanted to defend my best friend and tell my husband that he was wrong and being an asshole. Go off on him for being so cruel and callous, and tell him only a complete jerk would say something like that at a time like this. But he was right. And I knew it. So even though I wanted to stand up for her, like she'd done so many times in the past for me, I couldn't.

I tightened my grip on Jack's hand and allowed him to pull me outside where Matteo was waiting by the car. The heat and humidity smacked me square in the face and I sucked in one final breath before letting all the stress of the weekend go.

A couple of weeks later, I still couldn't believe what had happened between Melissa and Dean. Watching him lose his shit on her was the most I'd ever seen him act like Jack. And it was hot. I'd never admit that to Jack, but it really was. I was surprised Melissa's panties didn't melt off her body and into a puddle on my apartment floor. Instead, she dug in her heels and acted stubborn and defensive, which was her version of a defense mechanism, I supposed.

Truth be told, I was really sad for them. I wanted them to work it out and I had no idea why Melissa was fighting it so hard. What kind of person doesn't know what the hell was wrong with her best friend?

All I knew for sure was that I did not want to be in the middle of the two of them, so I bowed out; told them both I didn't want to be involved. True to their word, neither of them asked me about the other when we talked, which wasn't as often as it used to be. We'd all come so far from our college days in the student union.

Dean kept busy maintaining the office while Jack's agents, Marc and Ryan, traveled around the country scouting new baseball talent. It was Dean's job to be the local contact for potential talent. He took phone calls, handled the mail and the contracts, and filed scouting reports. He also kept tabs on new, upcoming, and past players, and was available in person at any time. Dean told me once that the only thing he didn't do was sleep there, but that could be arranged if they bought a couch. I laughed, but felt pride warm my heart at how hard he worked and loved the business.

Melissa, on the other hand, had convinced her mom to let her open a small extension of their public relations firm in Orange County. She informed her mother that over half their clients lived in the OC, and it didn't make any sense to force them to drive out to LA for in-person meetings. Their current clients were thrilled and word of mouth spread quickly about the new office location. Melissa found herself understaffed and her mom couldn't have been more proud of her only daughter. I always knew Melissa would run that place, so nothing she did surprised me.

Things with Jack and me had improved tremendously since he first got injured. He refocused all of his energy into working out and doing strength exercises in his opposite hand. When the team was on the road, he spent most of his time at the ball field with the team trainers. And when the team was home, he played pranks on all the guys during the games. They actually begged me to start keeping him home so he'd stop fucking with them.

I asked Jack over dinner one night what he was doing to torture his teammates and he couldn't stop laughing. He said, "I kept moving the new kid's gear in front of Newman's locker." I remembered that Newman was a veteran ball player, and if there was one thing that any first-year player had to do, it was respect the veterans. They weren't supposed to talk to them, let alone go anywhere near their stuff.

Jack leaned back and chuckled. "Newman was pissed and the poor kid had no idea how his shit kept getting there, but he couldn't say anything. Because, you know, he can't talk to a veteran player, and he certainly can't defend himself. Newman would take out all the crap in his bag, throw it across the locker room, and threaten the kid. I just kept doing it the whole weekend. Poor kid was about to lose his mind until someone told him, 'Welcome to the big leagues.'"

"Did they tell him it was you?" I smiled, happy to hear Jack laughing.

"Fuck no! No one tells him who is fucking with him. It's a rule. You play pranks, but you don't rat anyone out."

"Glad you're having fun with your teammates, babe." I smiled, reaching my hand across the table and touching the stubble on his cheek. I loved his scruff.

I will admit that having Jack home for dinner was really sort of nice. He'd never been around this much, and while his mind was definitely preoccupied with his injury, his physical presence was a welcome change. It made me realize how little he truly was home. And how rare it was for us to sit and have dinner together every night. That almost never happened.

Even during the off-season, Jack was always focused on what was to come. His mental state was all about working out, staying fit, eating right, and doing whatever had to be done to stay relevant and needed for the upcoming season. I honestly didn't mind the amount of his time that baseball took, but some moments, like the ones right now, it was nice to have him around.

Staring over at my sexy man, I stifled the urge to crawl across the table and eat him for dinner. I knew he wouldn't mind, but didn't want to stop the current conversation that flowed between us. Watching Jack smile and laugh had been the highlight of my day.

"So, tell me about the rookie they brought up to pitch for you," I said and his eyebrows lifted.

"Did I tell you he won't be staying?" He smirked and a dimple appeared. I wanted to get lost in that dimple.

I reached for my wineglass and took a sip. "Where's he going?"

"He's temporary," he said with a smirk.

"Who told you that?"

"He told me. Just walked up to me one night during a game and said, 'They told me not to get too comfortable here, you know.' Which, of course, I didn't know." Jack fumbled with his fork. "Fuck. I'll never get used to trying to eat with my right hand."

I laughed. "So, what did you say to him after that? Anything?"

"Fuck no, I didn't say anything. I just looked at him. I don't owe that kid anything. He'd take my position in a heartbeat if they let him. And I know that."

"So, he'll get sent back down to Triple-A when you're off the disabled list?" I asked before filling my mouth with a large helping of Caesar salad.

"I assume so. He's good, though. And I hate how much I hate that he's good. Makes me feel like a dick."

"You're not a dick. You worked your ass off to earn that position and you don't want it taken away from you." I understood that feeling. I knew how much baseball meant to Jack and how much he'd been through personally and professionally to achieve his goals. No one wanted to have one stupid incident be the catalyst for your entire career changing. Or for its loss.

"Exactly. But I want the team to win. And he helps them win. But then I'm pissed that he helped them win because sometimes I don't want him to be that good." He dragged his good hand through his hair, his mood suddenly shifting.

"It makes sense," I said encouragingly, trying to reassure him as his eyes lifted to meet mine. It was the team's job to win games at all costs. Jack was terrified he'd lose his position to a younger kid who threw faster than him. Every player's fear when they were injured was that they'd be replaced. Baseball made it known that there was a long line of younger guys waiting to take your spot the moment you screwed up. That was a lot of pressure.

My voice rose in pitch as my thoughts spilled from my mouth, my adrenaline kicking in. "You love your team. You don't ever want them to lose. But you don't want this kid to be better than you are because you want to be missed. You want to be needed. You want the goddamn Mets to be affected by your absence!"

Jack's eyes flew open wide and a huge smile lit up his face. "That's it! That's exactly fucking it. God, I love you."

The sound of his chair screeching across the tile floor hit my ears as quickly as Jack's hot mouth did. "You. Naked. Now."

My heart raced and the space between my legs ached with want. It never ceased to amaze me how easily Jack could turn me into a hot puddle of desire. One second we were laughing, and the next all I could think about was having him inside me.

I turned my head toward him as his mouth crushed against mine. He kissed me hard once, twice, then when I parted my lips, his tongue took advantage and searched for mine. The moment our tongues touched, my body ached and throbbed in unison.

"You're so hot," I managed to get out as he lifted me into his arms and carried me to the bedroom. I started to protest, concerned about his broken hand, but he silenced me with his mouth.

"Don't talk," he demanded and I obeyed. I'd do anything he asked right now, I was so turned on. "God, Cassie, I want you. You're so smart."

He kissed my neck and the feel of his lips made me dizzy. "And beautiful." He licked his way down my neck to my shoulder, where he bit gently and nibbled. I breathed out a heady moan and felt him twitch against me.

"And talented," he continued as he reached for the bottom of my top, lifting it up over my head and tossing it to the floor. He instantly moved his mouth to my bare stomach, where he kissed and licked around my belly button, the skin so sensitive there that I shivered.

"And made for me." His head lifted as his brown eyes met mine. "You know that, right?" His eyes narrowed as his right hand moved to unclasp my bra. "That you were literally fucking made for me? This body," he said, discarding my lacy bra onto the floor with my top, "this body was made for me. And only me. Tell me you know that."

Jack reached his hand toward my cheek and I closed my eyes, letting the heaviness of his words settle inside me. The space between us filled with so much love, lust, desire, and want, I felt like I could literally cut a piece out of the air and consume it. This moment could fill me … complete me … satisfy me. I could live forever from the emotions I felt in this one moment.

"Say it, Cassie. Tell me you know this body was made to fit with mine. And only mine. No rookie can take my place. No one else can have this position. You're my fucking wife and no one else's. Ever. I worship you. I will always worship you."

I didn't know why, but his words filled me with so much emotion, I almost started crying. Maybe it was the way he said them, or what was being said, but my chest heaved with each laboring breath I took. Overwhelmed, I looked at my husband. My sexy as hell, overly confident, amazingly beautiful husband. Looking at him now, like this, I felt reassured at just how lucky we were to have each other. I'd never want anyone else as long as I lived. It was Jack Fucking Carter for me, or no one.

"Say it, Kitten. Tell me you're mine," he demanded, his voice almost purring.

I sucked in a deep breath and watched as my exposed breasts rose and fell. Tangling my fingers in his dark hair, I tugged slightly, forcing his eyes to stay locked on mine. "I'm yours. There will never come a time when I don't belong to you. It's you for me, or no one. You hear me? Only you. Only yours. Forever."

Our feelings spilled out, replacing the oxygen in the room with something else entirely. Jack's words were like my own personal aphrodisiac, each one burning hotter between my legs than the last. I was a puddle of want, so completely turned on by everything he'd just confessed, I was surprised I didn't spontaneously combust and melt into the bed.

"Forever," he concurred before he moved his mouth to my chest. His tongue was frenzied as he flicked my pebbled nipple, before sucking it into his mouth and holding it between his teeth. I whimpered and he shivered. He sucked and licked before moving to the next one, giving it the same treatment.

I writhed underneath him, raising my hips to meet his, telling him with no words that I was ready to have him inside me.

"Not yet," he said to my silent plea. He moved his good hand toward my jeans, but fumbled with the button. "You gotta get these off, Kitten. I'm fucking useless with this hand."

I unbuttoned my jeans and lowered the zipper. Shimmying out of them, I watched as Jack did the same with his before discarding them on the floor. He paused for only a moment, but it was long enough for me to see him in all his naked glory. I wanted to freeze-frame this second and burn it into my memory. Naked Jack Carter was truly a sight to behold. From his chiseled shoulders and chest all the way down to the manhood that jutted from between his muscular thighs. This man's athletic body did a number on me.

I pursed my lips together and reached for his length, but he shook his head. His eyes met mine before he lowered his head between my legs. My lips parted as he kissed my inner thigh, slowly, methodically. He teased me until I felt like I didn't know how to breathe on my own. Every breath felt wrong, filled with too much effort. Who the hell has to *think* about breathing? Apparently I do when my husband is positioned between my thighs.

His tongue left a trail of wetness up my thigh and close to my sex before moving to the opposite leg. I wriggled and grabbed his head, trying to force him to focus his attention where I desperately wanted him to. He laughed. "Almost, Kitten," he said, his words hot against my skin.

Just when I thought I couldn't take any more and I considered actually killing him with my legs, his tongue found my sweet spot. My chest heaved as I released the air building within me. He licked me in soft strokes before becoming more focused, more feverish. The flicks of his tongue caused my frenzy to build as he moved from one area to another. One moment his tongue lapped at me, and the next it was diving inside of me, moving in and out in rapid succession.

I squeezed my eyes so hard I saw stars. Or maybe it was his mouth that made me see them. Who knew? All I knew for sure was that it was fucking magical. My husband was a magician with a wand for a tongue and I didn't care who knew.

"Jack. Oh God, Jack. Don't stop. Don't ever stop," I shouted. "You're like Harry Potter, oh God!"

Instantly, he stopped. Midlick, he lifted his face from between my legs to stare at me, and I swear I felt my vagina curl up and die a little.

"Did you just call me Harry Potter?" Jack's face twisted with humor and confusion.

"I just meant that you were magical. Your tongue is fucking magic. Get down there and perform a spell. Shut up, Jack. Just get back down there." I pushed his head as he laughed.

"He might be magic, but he's not real. I'm real. This is real." His tongue resumed its magical licking as he pushed two fingers inside me. My climax continued to build with each flick of his tongue and every thrust of his fingers.

"Just like that, Jack. Oh yes," I yelled as my hips twisted and jerked, my orgasm tearing through my body with force.

He pulled his head away from me slowly, a dimpled smile on his face. "Are you going to start calling me Harry?"

"Only if you want me to," I panted as he positioned himself on top of me and pushed inside. The size of him filled me up and I moved my hips in time with his.

"Fuck, Cassie. Always. You always feel so good." He pushed himself hard against me, reaching deeper with each thrust.

"Deeper, Jack. Go deeper," I begged as he grabbed my shoulders and rolled underneath me, never pulling out. I pushed my body on top of his, taking him in as deep as I could. Moving up and down, I leaned toward him, kissing his chest and licking around his nipple.

My hips continued to move, pumping him in and out of me as his erection grew with each stroke against its length.

"Do you feel that?" he asked, referring to his growing size. His voice was tight, as if he couldn't get enough air. "I'm gonna come, Kitten. I'm almost there."

I nodded as my own climax built within me. As I worked myself up and down along him in a hurried pace, he stiffened, reaching a place in me only he ever had, and I began to shudder. Jack's eyes closed as he exploded inside me, filling me up. I reveled in the thrill of his orgasm as another one of my own ripped through me. My body pulsed as my heartbeat throbbed in my ears. I collapsed onto Jack's chest and lay there panting as he ran his fingers through my hair, his breathing fast and his body slick with sweat.

"Mine," was all he said as he kissed my forehead. "Forever."

Traded

Jack

Three weeks later ...

Today marked six weeks since I'd broken my fingers. Cassie wanted to come with me to meet with the team doctor for moral support, but I told her I needed to do this alone. It had nothing to do with me wanting her there or not, but more to do with the fact that she couldn't do anything about the diagnosis.

If my fingers were healed, then that was great. But if they were still fucked up, she couldn't make them better, and I needed time to process that. This was the kind of thing a man went into alone and then thanked God, or whoever, that he wasn't alone when he came out. Cassie was great about it, completely understanding. But then again, my girl always had been.

She wished me good luck as she walked out the door for work, and I promised to call her as soon as I knew anything.

Nerves twisted inside my gut as the possibility of my career being over hung above my head like some sort of metaphorical rain cloud. I could barely eat or think of anything else as I hopped up on the exam table.

"How you feeling?" the doctor asked, all nonchalant, and I wanted to strangle him for attempting small talk with me at a time like this.

Unwilling to respond, I gave him a curt smile and a head nod instead. It was immature and unprofessional, but if he didn't get this cast off my arm and give me a prognosis, I was going to throw up all over his stupid shiny shoes.

He grabbed a weirdly shaped contraption and started to cut through my cast. Peeling away at the layers, he gently removed it. Waving off the rank smell that accompanied it, I grumbled an apology.

"Comes with the territory, Jack. No one can go six weeks without washing an area of their body and have it smell like roses," he explained.

He clearly didn't know my wife. I'd bet she could. She could do anything.

I looked at my arm, which was wrinkled and pale from being holed up for the last six weeks. I had to stop myself from hitting it to get the natural coloring to return. Holding my arms up side by side, my normally strong arm looked diseased and wasted.

"How long until it looks like my hand again?" I asked the doctor.

"That's all normal too. Now, let me see how your fingers look." He reached for my hand and asked me to straighten it. They were sore and underused.

"That's great, now make a fist."

I did as he asked, fisting my fingers into the palm of my

hand. Every movement felt foreign. And weak.

I was not used to being weak.

"It all looks good. The bones healed nice and straight. With about a week or so of rehab, Jack, you should be back on the mound, depending."

"Depending on what?" I asked sharply.

"No, no." He waved a hand in apology. "I just meant depending on how you feel, strength-wise. Everyone heals differently," he said and I exhaled.

"Can I throw today?" I asked, determined to heal as soon as possible and get back on the mound where I belonged.

"I don't see why not. Just take it easy."

I fired off a quick text to my girl.

Hand looks good. Everything healed well. Off to see how it feels.

My phone beeped out a response before I could put it down.

So relieved. And so thankful. Good luck, babe. I love you.

I walked into our private indoor batting cage and grabbed a ball. Palming it, I slowly wrapping my fingers around the seams in a curve-ball grip. I couldn't hold it as tightly as before, but I wasn't worried. One hundred percent healing would come with time. With my heart in my throat, I pulled my arm back and released the ball, not trying to pitch it, simply warming up.

It didn't feel the same. My grip was weak and my fingers

lacked the sheer strength they had a mere six weeks ago.

After winding my way back into the doc's office, I asked him, "Should I do strength exercises first? Get my finger and hand strength back?"

"Absolutely," he said as he tossed me a sponge-like ball. "Squeeze this." I did as he asked and he smiled. "Good. Now do that multiple times a day, but don't overdo it. No more than ten reps and no more than five times each day. I know it doesn't seem like much, but trust me. Also, make sure you flex your fingers and press them against something flat, like your table at home."

"All right, Doc. Thanks."

For the next week, I did as the doctor ordered, and each time I threw the ball at the field, I felt more and more like my old self. My hand felt good and when Coach clocked me, I threw between ninety and ninety-one consistently. Not as fast as before, but still fast. He removed me from the disabled list and told me I'd be closing out the next home series.

I couldn't wait to throw again. Or get in my full uniform. While I was hurt, I only had to wear my sliding pants and a pullover. I wanted to be dressed in full gear again.

Sunday afternoon, the stands of Shea stadium were packed, an almost sold-out crowd, I was told. There was something about an afternoon game in the summer. Everyone wanted to be there, watching our nation's favorite pastime.

When I took the mound, the cheers were deafening. I'd been missed. Thank God I'd been missed; I missed them too. The fans, the cheers, the stadium, the smell of the food cooking and the freshly mowed grass around me.

Stepping onto the mound, I scooted the dirt away from around the front edge with my toe, making a small divot. I kicked my cleat hard against the white rubber before turning to stand on it. It was crazy, but I'd missed the way my feet felt on the springy step.

The knowledge that I'd lost velocity on my pitches did little to soothe the anxiety that swirled inside me. I wanted to throw harder, pitch faster, get right back to where I was, but my hand wouldn't cooperate. My fingers weren't capable of gripping the ball as tightly as they once did. And when the baseball left my fingertips, the same force I once had, had lessened. I knew it because I felt it. From my arm all the way to my toes, my body reacted to the way my pitches had changed.

After sucking in a deep breath, I aimed at the catcher waiting for my warm-up pitch, and threw. The ball flew right down the center, a perfect fast-ball right down the pipe. My hand felt good and I wanted to keep it that way, so I stretched my fingers and threw ten more pitches before the first batter stepped up to the plate.

Aiming for the glove and agreeing to the catcher's call for a first pitch fast-ball on the outside corner, I pulled my arm back and threw. The batter swung and missed. I glanced at the scoreboard behind me to check my speed as I walked back to the mound. The numbers nine-zero showed on the screen under the strike one count.

Shit.

I could only imagine what the announcers were saying about me right now. A first-pitch fast-ball at only ninety miles an hour? Send this kid back to the minor leagues. Doing something I rarely fucking do, I stole a look toward where the players' wives sit and locked eyes with mine. Then I tipped my hat twice, my sign for my girl, and I could see the outline of her smile spread across her face.

Looking at her gave me the extra strength I needed to get through this. Then I remembered the necklace, and gave it a squeeze through my jersey. Taking a deep breath, I squinted toward the catcher. He flashed two fingers before tapping the inside of his thigh. I prayed my curve ball was still dirty as I fumbled with the seams of the ball to find my fingering. I lifted my knee into the air and hurled the ball toward the waiting batter, who swung and hit it right past me. My body arced out of the way of the incoming ball, the memory of being hit in the hand still fresh in my mind.

I kicked the dirt, and cursed in my head. Six weeks ago, that guy couldn't have hit my curve ball with a fucking Chevy. Now he hit it like I served it up on a platter for him. His timing was fucking perfect and mine was off.

The rest of the five innings I pitched were more of the same. I struck out four guys, and got most of the rest to ground out. But I was frustrated. I battled with myself, happy that I hit all my spots and threw a decent game, but angry that I couldn't throw faster. I tried and pushed myself as hard as I could, but I never threw over ninety-one.

When Coach pulled me, he patted me on the back and told

me not to worry about it. But I worried. In this sport, you always worry. Nothing was set in stone; you could always be replaced.

After the game, I walked through the familiar doors and into the hallway where Cassie waited for me. My girl calmed me. Her presence made everything okay. I could win any battle with her by my side. I'd go to fucking war if I knew I got to come home to her.

She leaned up on her toes and planted a wet kiss on my lips. "You did great. How do you feel?"

"Thanks, Kitten. I feel okay. I know I can do better."

"It's your first game back. You'll get stronger every outing."

"Every outing? Aw, you sound like a ball player already," I teased, throwing my arm around her back.

"But really, I mean it. No one expects you to be perfect right off the bat."

I knew she only tried to help, but I questioned her words. My coach, the team's manager, they did all expect that. Whether they said it to my face or not, they expected it, and they talked about it behind closed doors.

"Feed me, woman. I'm starving," I said to change the subject, and kissed the side of her head as we headed out of Shea.

The next month was more of the same as far as ball was concerned. I pitched every few games on rotation, but couldn't gain any speed or velocity in my pitches. Everyone kept talking about all the time I needed to get my full strength back, but I could see the disappointment in their eyes. And even though my teammates never admitted it to my face, they were all happy this wasn't happening to them. I couldn't blame them, though. If the situation were reversed, I'd be feeling the same way. Thankful it wasn't me.

From the outside, people probably thought of baseball as a simple sport. The general public thought that any athlete who made a living playing a sport should never have any cause for complaints. How lucky would we all be if we got paid a ton of money to play a game every day?

But life was rarely as simple as people imagined it was. Baseball was so much more than that. It was a business. And it was ugly sometimes. One of the most frustrating things to a player was when the business side of baseball came into play and messed with your desire to simply play the game.

All of us ball players just wanted to play the game. None of us wanted to be involved in the business side of it, that was why we had agents and managers. We were desperate for them to handle all of that so we could simply concentrate on playing our game.

But that wasn't how baseball worked. You played on their terms. You were a fucking pinball that could be hit, bumped around, knocked into a holding pen, good for some extra points, or go down the gutter when the flippers couldn't reach you. But you were still just a tiny ball on their playing field.

"Jimmy wants to see you," Coach told me after I'd showered. Nerves shot through me; it wasn't good if our team manager wanted to talk to me. I knew my game wasn't the same as it used to be, but I'd just gotten back. I wasn't a hundred percent yet and they knew that. I needed more time.

"Close the door, Jack," Jimmy's gruff voice demanded.

My stomach in knots, I closed the door and stood in front of it.

He waved me forward. "Come sit."

I shook my head. "I'd rather stand. If you're going to give me bad news, I'd rather not be sitting." I reached for my pitching hand and stretched my fingers back.

Jimmy nodded and looked me straight in the eye, his voice all business, no emotion. "Fine. Jack, look, we're going to be trading you. Two teams are asking for you and I wanted to ask your preference." He sat back and watched me, obviously waiting for a response.

Did he just say they were trading me?

My first instinct was to fight, but this wasn't the kind of thing you fight. It didn't work like that. Being traded wasn't a negotiation with your agent or your family or anyone. It was purely a team-to-team deal and you were usually left out of it. There was no contract to write up, since whatever team got you, also got your current contract. Usually players had no say in the matter. It was the rare case that they asked your opinion at all.

Like this one.

I wanted to fight, but I was too shocked to respond at first. The word "traded" kept banging around inside my head.

"But I love New York. And this team," I said, sounding so much like a child I immediately wanted to kick myself as soon as the words were out.

"We know you do, kid. But your pitches have lost something and it's in the team's best interest to make a trade."

The team's best interest.

Baseball is a business.

Baseball is a business.

Baseball is a business.

No matter how many times I reminded myself of that fact, it didn't lessen the sting.

Pressure built up in my chest as I looked away, struggling with what to say. Finally, I pulled myself together and stared steadily back at him. "I'm not healed a hundred percent yet. I just need more time. I'll get back to where I was, you know I will."

He shook his head. "It's already a done deal."

"Why do I get to choose where I go?" I felt a little dizzy as the room spun, or maybe it was my head, still reeling from the news.

"Because it's an even trade. Both teams are offering the same things, so I figured I'd do you the courtesy of asking if you had a preference where you went."

"Thank you," I said with a nod.

"Both Toronto and Anaheim are asking for you. You let me know which team you'd prefer, and I'll do my best to make it happen for you."

I sucked in a breath. It was a no-brainer. "Anaheim. Definitely Anaheim." If I had to get traded and move, the least I could do was take Cassie back home.

Shit.

Cassie was going to kill me.

My mind whirled with all the ramifications of this move. Cassie had a job she loved. We'd made a home here in New York. We were Matteo's only clients. We had friends, and responsibilities, and suddenly I felt like the weight of the world rested on my shoulders.

Jimmy cleared his throat. "Great. I'll let them know." He gave me a nod of dismissal and waved me toward the door.

I moved to leave but paused for a second, then turned around and asked, "When will it go through?"

"The deadline's in a few days, so not before then."

A few days?

"Will I throw any more for the team?" I asked. It was probably a weird question, but I liked knowing when something this momentous was going to be my last time. I wanted to be able to say good-bye, knowing I was kicking the mound for the last time, putting on the uniform for the last time, walking onto the field for the last time. I'm a baseball player; we're fucking mental, okay?

"Probably not. You're a good pitcher, Jack."

A few months ago I was a great pitcher.

"You still have some years left in you, so don't let this get you down. This is all part of the game."

I saw red for a second as emotions welled up within me at the injustice of it all. *Fucking easy for you to say.*

Lucky for me I didn't voice that thought out loud, but settled for muttering, "Not really."

"Excuse me?" Jimmy slammed his pen down on the desk and eyed me, his face slowly turning red.

"This," I said tersely, then paused. "This isn't part of the game at all. It might be part of the *business*, but it's not part of the game." Then I opened the door and walked out.

Still had a few years left in me? I'd show them. My hand wasn't fully healed yet, and I could still come back just as strong as I was before. The Mets organization might have just quit on me, but I refused to. I'd play my best years for the Anaheim Angels. At least I would still be playing.

Matteo drove me home in silence. It had been like that since I'd gotten hurt. He let me take the lead when it came to my wanting to talk or not, and most days lately, I'd been silent. I felt like a shitty person because we were friends; I just didn't always act like one lately.

"See you later. Thanks for the ride," I said as I hopped out of the car before he could, and headed into my building.

Upstairs, I walked through our front door, desperate for my girl. "Cassie?" I yelled into the silence and waited. No response. She didn't go to the game this afternoon because she had to work and I wasn't pitching.

Glancing at my cell phone, I realized she was probably still at her office. I couldn't wait; I'd go fucking insane if I didn't talk to her. She needed to know what was happening and I needed to tell her sooner rather than later.

There was no later. We'd have to leave New York in just a few short days.

I dialed her phone and paced the floor as I waited for her to pick up.

"Hey, babe," she said, her voice a soothing balm on my shattered nerves.

"Kitten, what time will you be home tonight?" I tried to hide the urgency in my tone, but failed.

"Why?" she asked sharply, immediately on high alert. "Are you okay? I can leave right now if you need me to."

"Yes. I need you to," I admitted.

"Is everything okay? Are you okay?" she asked, the worry in her tone heartbreaking.

I tugged at my hair as I paced. "I'm fine, I promise. I just need you to come home."

"Okay. I'll be right there."

I paced a fucking hole in the floor the fifteen minutes it took Cassie to walk through our door. The second she did, I practically sprinted to her and pulled her into my arms. "I'm sorry. I'm so sorry."

"What's going on? Jack, you're scaring me," she confessed, her face draining of color.

"I'm getting traded," I blurted out.

Any of the remaining pink in her cheeks instantly vanished. "W-where?"

"They asked me if I had a preference and I said yes, but I won't know until the trade goes through."

"Where?" she asked again, her tone more demanding this time.

"Either Anaheim or Toronto."

"Okay. Okay." Her eyes lost focus for a second, then the rapid-fire questions began. "So then what? We have to move, right? And get rid of this place. Do you help me move? Of course you don't. How does this work?" She paused, the wheels in her head clicking and turning clear as day, then realization set in. "I have to quit my job. Oh my God. I love my job."

I wanted to fix it. Fix every single thing for her. Tell her she never had to quit anything for me. Or move for me. Or change her life in any possible way for me, but I'd die without her. I needed this girl the way plants needed oxygen. So I could tell her all of those things, but I'd be lying through my teeth. And she'd know it.

Cassie looked at me, her green eyes bright with tears. "How does this work? Tell me what this means."

The look on her face broke my heart. I pulled her toward the couch and onto my lap, then wrapped my arms around her. I'd tell her anything she wanted to hear, but first I needed to feel her close to me. I needed to be touching her while I did it.

I pressed my head against her rib cage. "I have to leave the night the trade goes through. Whenever that is and wherever we are. The game will end and they'll hand me a plane ticket."

"What if you're on the road?" she asked, playing with the strands of my hair.

"Then I leave from there. I don't get to come home and see you or pack or anything like that. If we're on a road trip, I leave straight from the road to meet up with the other team, wherever they are."

"That's harsh," she said and I laughed.

"It is kinda harsh."

She sucked in a deep breath. "And you don't get any time off, right? I mean, you guys only get forty-eight hours when your wives have babies, so you wouldn't get time off for this."

"No, I don't get any time off. But that doesn't mean you have to do all this alone. You can talk to your boss, and make a plan. You don't have to come with me right away. If we wait until the off-season, I can help you pack and we can move together."

Cassie thought for a moment, then said, "Jack, look at me," her voice soft and comforting as I glanced up. "I'm not going to stay here without you. You get traded, I get traded. We're a team, remember?"

Hugging her tight, I spoke against her hair. "I just don't want you to feel like you're all alone in this. I completely understand if you want to wait until I can help. And if you need time to transition from your job to our new home, take all the time you need." And I meant every word. It would fucking kill me to be without her, but she had a life here too. It was only fair she left it on her own terms.

She sniffed, then snuggled in closer to me. "I don't want you to worry about me. I can handle moving and everything else that goes with it. You just worry about getting on that new team and showing the Mets that they screwed up by letting you go. I can't believe they're trading you!"

"Thank you, Kitten. I can't believe it either. Good thing I still have this necklace. I think I'm gonna need it." I pulled the key from under my shirt and stroked the letters stamped on it before letting it fall against my chest.

"It's yours. Until you don't need it anymore," she said with a smile as she reached her hand out to touch it. "I feel betrayed by the team, in a way. Why do I feel like that? Do you feel like that?"

What I did feel was fucking stupid for having hurt feelings over this. What was I, a twelve-year-old? No, I was a man and grown men weren't supposed to get butt-hurt over shit like this.

But truth be told, I was hurt. And I hated to admit it, but I vowed to never lie to my wife again and I took that seriously. "I don't know that I feel betrayed as much as I feel let down. Like, I guess I stupidly thought they'd fight for me. Just because my pitching isn't up to par right now, that they would know it would be back eventually. I feel like they quit on me. And it hurts because I'd never quit on them. They're my team and I always give a hundred and ten percent when I'm on that mound. It hurts knowing it's not a two-way street. Is that stupid?"

Yeah, I felt stupid admitting all this to her. Even though I knew she understood me more than anyone else in this world, it still sucked saying it all out loud.

"It's not stupid at all," Cassie said loyally. "You love this team. And it's like you just got told they don't love you the same way back. They broke up with you."

I snorted. "I got dumped."

Then she looked up at me with those big fucking green eyes and said, "I'll never dump you."

My heart full of love for her, I reached for her left hand and kissed the diamond I'd bought her. "I wouldn't let you."

She laughed, her body shaking against mine. "Yeah, I know. Been there, done that."

"And look how well that turned out," I teased playfully, knowing damn well she was the best thing to ever happen to me.

"I'd say it turned out better than well, Mr. Carter."

"For me, maybe. I don't know about your end of the deal."

Slightly Emotional

Cassie

Jack got the news he'd been traded to Anaheim two days later. The Mets were in St. Louis and just like he said, he had to fly straight from there to Texas to meet up with his new team, the Anaheim Angels. Of course they went by some other name now, but growing up in Southern California, they'd always be the Anaheim Angels to me.

We really lucked out that the Angels were one of the teams fighting for Jack. That meant we got to move home, and it also meant that Jack didn't have to try to find a place to live in his downtime. Grateful we had family in the area, he moved straight in with Gran and Gramps until I got there.

If he had been traded to Toronto, the team would have put him in a hotel for the first home stand only. It would only be for a few nights, then he would have had to find permanent accommodations on his own. That was just another harsh reality of playing professional baseball. No one helped you when you needed help the most. If Jack didn't have me, I couldn't imagine what he'd do. The players didn't have time to find places to live, and deal with other necessary issues like that, when their entire days were spent at the ball field trying to maintain their position.

Of course I hated the idea of leaving work and the home we'd created in New York, but I hated being away from Jack's home base even more. So I knocked on Nora's door the morning after the trade.

"Hmph. I know why you're in my office," she said, momentarily pretending to be offended with me. Then real indignation took over. "I can't believe they traded him!"

Taken aback, I didn't know whether to laugh or cry. "I feel the same way."

"I'm really going to miss you," she said, her face solemn. Nora was a smart woman; she'd obviously put two and two together to figure out why I'd come to meet with her unannounced.

"And I can't believe I have to move back to California. Don't get me wrong, I love my home, but I'm not ready to say good-bye to New York yet. Is that bad?"

"Of course not. New York's in your blood, Cassie. Plus, I have a proposition for you." She rubbed her hands together and a devious smile appeared.

My mood immediately lifted. "What is it? Please let it be something that means I can still work here but not physically be here," I practically begged.

She huffed and glared at me, shaking her head. "You ruin every surprise."

"Tell me!"

"As long as you can deal with being an independent contractor instead of an employee, I can hire you on a project-by-project basis. And darling, your work more than speaks for itself, so I have no problem in doing just that."

I stood up from my chair and ran to the other side of Nora's desk, then reached down and squeezed her hard. "Thank you so much, Nora! Thank you, thank you, thank you, thank you!" I exclaimed into her hair. "This means everything to me."

"Honey, we're lucky to have you."

"No, I'm lucky to have you," I practically shouted. "When should I do the switch? And how will it work?"

"I assume you need to move as soon as possible, am I right?" she asked and I shrugged. "I can't promise you work all the time, but I will get you whatever I can. It won't be like it is now, but it's better than nothing. And since you'll be an independent contractor, you can charge me per hour or a flat fee, that's something you'll need to figure out on your own. But the money can potentially turn out to be the same for less work, technically speaking."

"I seriously love you."

"Great. Now, go type up your letter of resignation and hand it in so I can let you go."

"You're going to make me cry," I said, wiping at the tears threatening to fall.

"I'm trying to make your life easier, Cassie, not make you cry." She tormented me with a knowing glance.

"You're right. And I love you for it. I can never thank you enough, Nora. You've been the best boss in the world."

She nodded and admitted with no shame, "I am pretty amazing."

I burst out laughing. "I had no idea what I was going to do, or how I was going to leave. Thank you for making this so easy for us."

Nora let out a little huff. "It's your own fault for being so damn talented. Now go," she said with a dismissive wave, "before you mess up my mascara."

I gave Nora another hug, kissed the side of her cheek, and turned to walk out of her office for the last time in the foreseeable future.

"By the way," she said, "the photos you took of Trina are incredible. You still want to shoot her post-pictorial, right?"

"Absolutely! Trina would kill me." Inside, I reveled at the fact that I'd get to come back here in the near future to work. I wasn't even gone yet, but I already longed to be back. New York City had definitely left its mark on me.

Closing Nora's door behind me, I walked to my desk for the last time. I sat down and spun my chair around to stare at my computer screen, looking over the letter of resignation I'd already typed out for two seconds before e-mailing it over. If I looked at it for too long, I might be tempted to press DELETE.

Thankfully, or oddly, depending on how you looked at it, I had only acquired a small amount of personal belongings over the years. I scooped them up and slipped out of the office, then pressed the DOWN elevator button without making a fuss. Just the thought of leaving was hard enough; I didn't want to make a spectacle out of it. I planned on sending a good-bye e-mail to the office once I was settled back in California.

I know, I know, it was sort of a chicken-shit move, but the reality was that co-workers didn't let people leave easily. They had a habit of creating chaos and parties and celebrations that never ended. It was all with good intentions, but I didn't have time for that. I needed to get our belongings packed and moved out to Los Angeles as soon as possible. Jack and I needed a new home, and it was my job to find us one. Because that was what the wife of a major league baseball player did. She took care of her man.

As I walked up the street toward the subway station, I thought I'd be more emotional. I actually braced myself for the tears and soul ache that never came. I'd fought so hard with Jack about having my own career, and had taken such a strong stand when it came to what I dreamed and wanted. But right now, all I truly wanted was to be home with my husband. I knew I told Jack exactly that the other night, but that was before I'd quit, before I'd actually resigned from my job.

Passion was a fickle thing. It could make you think you'd die for something one minute, then force you to realize you'd be just fine without it the next. A year and a half ago, I would have sworn on my life that I couldn't survive a single moment if I didn't have my career. Take away photography, and I assumed my soul would wither and die on the spot, leaving nothing but a memory of what once was.

But life had a way of changing your priorities. Or maybe it was me that had changed, because I'd never felt more full of life than I did right now. And none of it had to do with my career.

It was in this moment of truth, as I stood in a darkening subway station surrounded by strangers and lonely musicians, when I realized that my home was wherever Jack was. And he was no longer in New York, so I no longer belonged here. It was a simple truth, yet utterly profound in its message. I was meant to land wherever he settled, like the ocean washing seashells onto the shore. Jack was the shell, in constant motion and movement, being tossed around from place to place by the ebb and flow of something more powerful than he. And I was the sand, gripping and holding on to him, comforting his tumble with each push and pull of the tide, yet always constant.

When I walked into the waiting subway car, I had a smile plastered on my face. This understanding … this awakening … filled me with more joy than I'd ever considered possible. The best part was the acute awareness I had been given. It was like a gift. My heart wanted to burst with the sheer happiness I felt in this moment.

Before, I'd honestly never thought that following Jack's career would ever *feel* okay to me. I had figured that I would always be fighting to keep hold of something that I felt defined me in ways that were separate from Jack. But the thing was, Jack was a part of me, and choosing to keep our family together was an okay priority for me to have.

Not only was I the wife of a major league baseball player, but I was the wife of Jack Fucking Carter. And I wanted to take care of my man, the same way he chose to take care of me. There wasn't a doubt in my mind that Jack would do anything for me if I asked him to. The thing was, I had nothing I wanted to ask. Not anymore.

My fears in our relationship had been settled long ago. The point I tried to prove to him, to myself, had been proven. It wasn't giving up on my dreams to be there and support Jack. Somewhere along the line in our relationship, Jack and his life had become a part of my dreams too. Being with him fulfilled me in ways I'd only fought against before.

The simple truth was that it hurt a lot more to be away from Jack than it did to walk away from work. No one was more surprised by this revelation than me.

About an hour after I arrived home, the doorman called to let me know the packing boxes I'd ordered had arrived. Thankfully, he hauled them up for me and brought them in, stacking them higher than my kitchen table.

"Do you need packing tape, Mrs. Carter?"

I looked around and tapped the side of my head. "Probably. Do you have any I can borrow?"

He smiled, and his bushy eyebrows squished together like a giant gray caterpillar. "We have plenty. I'll be right back."

"Thank you, Thomas! Just walk back in," I yelled.

Jack had been right. Trying to do this all alone royally sucked. I looked around at all the things we'd acquired over the years, and realized there was no way I could do this alone, and in a short time frame.

How did the other wives do this, especially when they had kids? They had to have hired help, right? An idea forming, I dialed Trina's number and waited.

Thomas popped his head back in, dropped two tape guns on the table, and waved before letting himself back out. I mouthed "thank you" to him as Trina answered.

"I cannot believe you're leaving me," she said without

preamble, her accented voice startling me as she dove right in without saying hello.

I sighed. "I know. I'm trying not to think about it." Leaving Trina and Matteo was going to be hard. Maybe I could convince them to move with us? After all, we could use a driver in LA. As wonderful as it would be for us, I shook away the absurd idea.

"So, what's the matter? I know you're not just calling to chat this chubby girl's ear off."

"Trina, you're seven months pregnant! You're not chubby! You can't even tell you're pregnant from behind. Which, by the way, is why girls hate you."

"Girls hate me?" she scoffed, horrified at the very idea.

"I mean. If they did. That would be why," I said with a laugh.

"So, what's up, lovie?"

"When I move, can I call you anytime I want so you'll talk to me? You can read me the phone book, I don't care. I am going to miss hearing your voice so much."

Trina's British accent was absolutely precious; I might have developed a girl crush on her for that alone. Plus, the words she used were adorable. Everything was "brilliant" or "lovely;" when she was really sad or upset, she was "gutted;" and I was still trying to figure out what she meant by "gobsmacked." I thought it meant "shocked," but I'd never been sure.

"Only until the baby comes and then I'll probably put a hit on you if you wake me," she said with a giggle.

"Deal. So, the real reason I'm calling is because I don't know how I'm supposed to pack up this entire apartment by myself. I'm literally freaking out here, because there's no way I can do this alone. How do the other wives do it? What do people do? Help me!"

"You must be joking. Cassie, tell me you aren't sitting at home surrounded by a bunch of empty boxes wondering where to start?"

Turning my head slowly, I scanned our beautifully decorated apartment, looking at everything with a newly critical eye. Suddenly everything I'd carefully purchased and placed there with so much love looked like the bane of my existence. "Actually, I'm staring at a stack of boxes that still need to be built. Then I can surround myself with them and wonder where to start."

She tsk-tsked me before adding, "That will take you months to do by yourself. You have to hire movers, luv. They'll come pack your things and then drive them across the country for you. You just tell them where to deliver it all."

I sat up straight, excited at the very thought. "They'll pack for me? Shut the front door."

"Shut the front door? I'm going to remember that one," she teased. "But yes. You should call your contact in the Mets office and ask if they have anyone they recommend. They really should help you with this, Cassie, but I know that they sometimes won't. If you hit a dead end with them, get the number for your contact person in Anaheim and beg them for help. One of the goddamn teams should help the poor wife who gets stuck doing all the shit work."

I nodded, even though she couldn't see me. "I know, right? It's really insane to me that Jack gets traded while he's on the road. He can't come home. He has to leave with whatever he has packed, and then I'm supposed to handle moving our entire house across the country because he still has eight more weeks of baseball to play."

"That was one of the things that always killed me with Kyle. I know that I was on the road a lot, but I didn't have to take every modeling shoot that came my way. But those guys," she paused, as if disappointed somehow. "They don't get any time off for anything. Kyle used to tell me how sad the players on the team would get who were dads, you know?"

Huh? "No, I don't know. Tell me."

"Oh, just that the dads on the team were always really sad. He said they felt like absentee fathers all the time because of everything they missed. You know, like birthdays and holidays, and all the things that are important to little kids they always miss out on."

"Yeah, I've heard a few of the wives say things like that before. It's a brutal business. You have to really love the sport to want to play it that bad."

My eyes landed on a mason jar filled with quarters sitting on a shelf. I stared at it while Trina's voice filtered into my head, as my attention wandered slightly.

"And you have to really love the man playing it to want to stay with them through it all," she offered, giving me a compliment.

"It's either love or all the wives are crazy. Probably the latter."

"Probably." She yawned, which forced me to yawn in

response. "Sorry. I'm exhausted. This last trimester is kicking my ass. I'm tired all the time."

"You go. Thank you for the advice. I'll figure out what I need to do tomorrow. I'm really tired too. I'll blame you."

"Sympathy tiredness?"

"Yeah! I'm tired for you and your baby through the phone," I teased.

"Love you," she said, then yawned again.

"You too. 'Night."

Once you're no longer a part of an organization, you cease being their responsibility, or their problem. The Mets offered me nothing in the form of help or suggestions, and when I finally got off the phone with my contact there, I wanted to cry. The fact that I'd left a message for her that morning, then sat around all day waiting for a response and she didn't return my call until late that evening, probably had a lot to do with it.

I was so emotional lately, everything had me on edge. Of course, I blamed my overly delicate nature on Jack being gone all the time. But when a freaking tissue commercial caused me to burst into tears, I was convinced I'd gone crazy.

My cell phone rang and Jack's dimpled grin flashed across my screen. "Hello," I whined, wiping my nose with the back of my hand.

"Cassie? Are you crying? Why are you crying?" Jack's warm tone instantly turned protective.

"Nothing, babe. It's just this stupid commercial where this guy comes home from the war and sees his family and they don't know he's coming and he surprises them—" I cut off, tears falling in full force again.

"You're crying because of a commercial? Did I hear you right?"

I sniffed. "Shut up, Jack. I'm crying because I'm emotional. You're not here and I miss you so much. Our apartment is huge and we have a lot of shit and no one is helping me and all I want to do is be with you. But at this rate, I'll be here until next season."

"Ahhhh, Kitten." He started to laugh and I swore I'd kill him if he didn't stop. "Do you want me to send someone there to pack our shit? I'll fly you out to Seattle right now and I'll get someone to handle all that. You just say the word and it's done. You don't need to be doing that all alone. I told you that."

"That's so hot," I mumbled through my whimpering.

"What is?"

"The way you protect me and want to take care of me. I love youuuu," I told him, my declaration dragged out with my sobs. I couldn't stop.

"I love you too," he said. "Stop packing or not packing. Whatever you're doing, just stop. We'll figure it out later. But right now, we need to book my kitten a flight to come see me."

I sucked in a shaky breath. "Okay. That sounds good."

"We really don't have to move out right now, you know. Hell, we can keep the apartment in New York for all I care. We'll just never use it as often as we'll want to. But if you want to keep it, we should."

"I do want to," I said. "But then again I don't. It's not realistic and it's a waste of money."

"Your decision. I'll support whatever you want, okay? I just want you to be happy."

"I am happy," I cried out.

"I can tell," he said, his voice all funny like it was when he tried not to laugh. "Okay, babe, I have a ticket for you to fly out to Seattle first thing tomorrow morning. It's real early, so you need to go to bed. I'm e-mailing you and Matteo the itinerary now."

"How did you do that already? We're still on the phone."

"I'm Harry Potter, remember? I'm fucking magic!"

I laughed and he chuckled into my ear. "There's my girl. I'll see you tomorrow. Now, go get some sleep."

"Thank you. I miss you," I confessed with my whole heart, wishing he could feel just how deeply I meant the words. My love for Jack felt like it filled my body to bursting at every seam that held me together. I was overcome with emotion on every level.

"I miss you too. I hate being away from you. I've always hated it, but this is different. You're not home when I get there and it makes me crazy."

"Me too."

"Stop crying, please. It fucking kills me to hear you crying."

"I don't know what's wrong with me."

"You've finally cracked. I always knew you were crazy. I mean, I did get you to marry me."

I wiped my eyes, and couldn't stop the smile that formed on my face. "I'm in bed. I'll see you tomorrow."

"Good girl. I can't wait."

My plane landed in Seattle a little before eight the next morning. We disembarked via air stairs and walked across the paved runway before entering an annexed building. I glanced up at the clouds hovering in the sky. They threatened to drown me with the raindrops they carried. The air held a gentle chill that New York lacked this time of year. Even in a summer rainstorm, the East Coast air was hot and sticky. Not so in the Pacific Northwest. It was quite a change for me.

I walked through the small building, took the escalator down, and waited patiently for the shuttle that would take me to baggage claim. Within seconds, the double doors opened and I stepped inside. My stomach flipped as nervous energy surged through me at the idea of seeing my husband. I missed him so much.

Following the signs that pointed to baggage claim, I realized that I'd walked in a circle. Somewhere along the line, I wasn't translating the arrow directions correctly. Passing by the women's bathroom one more time, I decided I couldn't hold it and stepped inside. My stomach ached and fought against the urge to puke.

I must be hungry.

I splashed some cold water on my face before patting it dry with a paper towel. Stepping into the oncoming foot traffic, I decided to follow the herd of other travelers, convinced they would lead me straight to my destination. And they did.

When I was halfway down the escalator, I saw my husband standing at the bottom with a dimpled smile on his face, holding a sign that read:

LOST KITTEN
RETURN TO OWNER
REWARD IF FOUND
(FIFTY CENTS)

I covered my face with my hands and burst into tears. My mind flashed back to Jack in the airport when we first dated, holding the sign that read:

ANYONE SEEN
MY KITTEN?

I bolted from the escalator and straight into his waiting arms. His body was warm and comforting as he held me close.

"It wasn't supposed to make you cry." He kissed my head and patted my hair.

"The sign, Jack. The sign," I blubbered into his T-shirt. "And I've really missed you."

Holy hell, I need to stop crying all the time lately. Something is seriously wrong with me. I feel so out of control and unbalanced.

Jack's thumb reached across my cheek and wiped my tears away. He leaned down, pressing his lips against mine, and my body melted into his. "I've missed you too. Let's get your bag and get out of here."

I nodded as he linked his fingers with mine. "How's your hand feeling?"

"Good. Real good." While we waited at the baggage claim carousel, he flexed and stretched his left hand before reaching for my small suitcase. "This it?" he asked as he pulled it off the spinning track.

"Yeah, just that."

I don't know why I checked it when it was small enough to carry on board. Occupational habit, maybe. Whenever I traveled for work, I always checked all my equipment and bags, so this routine was second nature to me.

"I'm getting stronger, you know," he said, his eyebrows raised.

I flashed him a smile and squeezed his hand. "I knew you would."

"And I gained another mile per hour on my fast-ball yesterday." He grinned from ear to ear and my body heated with pride.

"Jack, that's fantastic. I'm so proud of you."

"Thanks, Kitten." His face beamed with pleasure, the light

brown rings closest to his pupils nearly glowing.

By the time we arrived at his hotel, my stomach betrayed me. I could barely stand up straight, it hurt so badly. I couldn't believe this was happening. I hadn't seen Jack in almost two weeks and now that we were together, I was sick?

"I'm sorry, Jack. I don't know what's wrong with me." I looked at him apologetically as we waited for the elevator.

"Don't be sorry, just get better. Did you eat breakfast this morning?"

I shook my head, the very idea of food making me want to hurl. "No. No food."

"I'll order—" he started to respond before I cut him off.

"No! I don't want anything!" I fought to keep the nothing I'd eaten inside my body as the elevator rocked to a stop. I wrapped my arm across my tummy and attempted to walk.

"I got you," Jack said before scooping me into his arms and carrying me down the long hallway. The last time he held me like this was after I'd gotten mugged in college. Some guy had come out of nowhere and stolen my camera and beat the crap out of me. When Jack finally found me, he picked me up and walked all the way to my apartment without stopping to catch his breath or slow his pace. It was the most romantic thing ever.

He was doing the same thing now. I leaned my body into his, listening to the sound of his heart beating against his muscled chest. It seemed like we walked for hours before we arrived at his hotel room door.

"I have to put you down," he warned before placing my feet gently on the ground. "Can you stand?"

"Yeah," I responded, my body doubled over in pain.

He swiped his keycard, the light turned green, and the lock made a clicking sound. Jack turned the handle and held the door open with his foot as I trudged inside. I rounded the corner and fell on top of his bed, pulling my knees to my chest.

"Kitten, what happened?" he asked as he sat down next to me on the bed. He propped pillows up behind him before pulling my head on top of his legs. His fingers ran through my hair and I could feel the intensity of his stare on me.

"Honestly, I'm not sure. I just don't feel good all of a sudden."

"I have to leave in two hours for the field, but I don't want to leave you like this."

"I'm sure I'll be fine after I nap or something. Don't worry about me."

He let out a loud huff. "Don't worry about you? Okay, Kitten. Sure thing. Never gonna fucking happen."

"I just meant that I'll be fine. I probably just need sleep and food." I hesitated. "At some point."

He stroked my hair, then stood up to walk over to the windows and pulled the curtains closed.

A moment later, he pressed a kiss to my cheek. Then he was gone.

My eyes opened in the darkened room, and when I turned my head to look for the alarm clock, my neck stiffened under the weight of my twisted sleeping position. How long had I been asleep?

"Jack?"

I moved my arm and the sound of paper crinkling drew my attention toward a piece of paper lying on the bedspread. It was a note from Jack.

Didn't want to wake you. I hope you feel better. Your tickets are at will-call, but please don't come if you don't feel good. I mean it, Kitten. If you feel like shit, stay here! I'll be back before you know it.

Determined to attend his game, I pushed myself to my feet. My head spun and I pressed my hand against the wall for balance. I needed water, and I knew Jack's mini fridge would be filled with it.

Opening a bottle, I took a sip before immediately bolting to the bathroom. The water I'd just swallowed came surging back up with a vengeance. Okay, I was definitely sick. There was no way I could go to the game like this; I'd never make it through a single inning.

Reaching for my cell phone, I typed out a message to Jack, letting him know I wouldn't be at the game. He wouldn't get to read it until after, but at least he'd know not to look for me and would come straight back to the hotel. Hopefully by then I'd be feeling better.

I set my phone on the bed beside me just as it rang. Melissa's singsong ringtone filled the room and I pressed OKAY to answer the call.

"Hey, girly," I whined into the phone line.

"Holy shit, you sound like death. Where are you?" Her chipper tone was almost too much for me to take in my current state.

"I'm in Seattle with Jack. Where are you?"

"Uh," she stuttered. "I'm at home. Where else would I be?"

I reached for a pillow and tucked it in front of my hips and tummy. Leaning my body against the coolness of the pillowcase helped settle my upset belly. "I don't know. So, what's up?"

"Why do you sound so bad? Are you sick?"

"I think so. My stomach is killing me and I threw up right before you called."

"Pregnant," she stated in her typical teasing tone, but something in that one word caused my breath to hitch.

When the hell was the last time I had my period? Was it over a month ago? I can't remember.

"Cass?" Melissa's voice rang in my ear.

"Sorry, I'm here. Shit, Meli, you might be right."

"I was totally joking."

Intrigued by the idea, I sat up and leaned back against the plush headboard. "I know you were, but I've been really tired lately. Not to mention, stupid emotional. Like, I cry at everything!" I complained.

"Everything?" she droned, mocking my confession.

"Everything!" I said forcefully. "Commercials. A fucking tissue commercial wrecked me the other day. I had to go to bed to stop thinking about it."

Melissa laughed hysterically on the other end of the line. I wanted to reach through the phone and smack her. "Oh, holy shit. You totally are pregnant."

"Meli, I have to go. I'll call you back." I hung up before she could respond and forced myself out of bed.

I needed to find a drugstore of some sort and buy some home pregnancy tests. Unless the hotel sold them, which I highly doubted. And the last thing I wanted was to run into a player's wife or girlfriend while I was buying something like that.

Like an idiot, I talked to my stomach, telling it to settle down enough to let me find a store. And then I promised it that if it let me not be sick until I got back to the hotel room, I'd let it make me sick all night if it wanted. I really needed to be able to find a store, buy some tests, and not puke while doing it.

Luck was definitely on my side because there was a drugstore right across the street from the hotel. I'd never purchased a pregnancy test before, so was surprised to find an entire aisle filled with shelves of them. I decided right then and there that there was definitely such a thing as too many options. There were plus signs, pink or blue, one line or two, yes or no, results before your first missed period or after, and more. My head spun and I had no idea which one was the best to buy. So I purchased four.

I raced back to the hotel, my ridiculous amount of pregnancy tests stuffed into a paper bag. Closing the door behind me, I removed the first box. I read the directions twice before attempting to follow them. The first time, instead of peeing on the damn stick, I peed all over my fingers. I wondered what kind of woman could control the direction of her pee the way the directions seemed to expect we could.

After washing my hands, I hurried into the living area and found my bottle of water. I chugged the whole thing to give myself plenty of ammunition before scooting back into the bathroom.

"Let's try this again," I said out loud, giving myself a pep talk.

Miraculously peeing on the proper part of the stick instead of my hands, I set the test on top of the sink counter and poured the rest of the tests out of the bag. They all informed me that they weren't one hundred percent accurate, so I should take more than one before going to a doctor for final confirmation.

Cell phone in hand, I stared at it, willing the minutes to go by faster. Unable to wait any longer, I wandered back into the bathroom and glanced down at the test, which was changing as I watched. The first window darkened and two lines appeared. It stated on the test that one line meant you were not pregnant and two lines meant you were. But it said nothing about a faint line. What did a barely there second line mean?

I scanned the directions and focused on the Frequently Asked Questions. It stated that the appearance of a second line meant that you were pregnant, no matter how faint or dark the line.

Pregnant.

Not willing to trust the one test, I took two more. All three yielded the same results:

PREGNANT.

Oh my gosh. I couldn't wait to tell Jack. He'd wanted to knock me up since the night he proposed. I fought the urge to call Melissa back and tell her, dying to share my news with my best friend. But Jack deserved to be the first person to know.

I laughed out loud when I realized why I'd been such a crazy freak lately. Thank heaven I had a reason for my incessant sob fests. I wasn't going insane, I was just pregnant.

With a baby.

In my belly.

Holy shit.

What if I turn out to be a crappy mom? I wonder how far along I am?

I hid the tests in the closet and fell asleep waiting for Jack to come back. When the door burst open, I jumped, the sound scaring me half to death.

"Sorry, Kitten! My hands are full, that's why I kicked the living shit out of the door here." Jack appeared, his arms filled with what looked like grocery bags.

"What is all that?"

"I got you ginger ale for your stomach, plus a bunch of other stuff in case you don't feel well. And then I got you a bunch of munchies and snacks in case you do. Do you feel better?"

"Much. How was the game?"

He grinned. "We won."

"Did you throw?"

"Not until tomorrow, you know that." He narrowed his eyes, looking at me closely before saying, "You're acting weird."

Jack couldn't possibly know anything. I wasn't acting weird; I was acting just like I always act.

Forcing an innocent look on my face, I asked, "How am I acting weird?"

"You have this look on your face. And your eyes …"

"What about them?"

He ran his thumb down the side of my face. "They're hiding something, but they want to share," he said as he lifted his eyebrows at me.

That's it. He is magic. I knew it.

About to burst with excitement, I couldn't stall any longer. "I don't know how you knew that, but I do have something to tell you. It has to do with why I wasn't feeling well earlier." I pulled him toward the closet. "The reason's in there."

"Is there a guy in the closet?" He stepped back, his hands balling into fists. "There better not be a fucking guy in this closet."

"What? No? I just hid something in here." I rolled the door open and pulled one of the tests down from the shelf. Unfolding the washcloth from around it, I presented it to Jack like a crown jewel on a display pillow.

He peeked down at the test stick, his brow furrowing. "What is tha—" He stopped midsentence, his eyes huge. "Is this? Are you?" He looked at me, his face full of wonder, and I nodded.

Jack fell to his knees and pressed his head against my belly. He wrapped his arms around me and held on to me without saying a word, his breath hot through the fabric of my shirt. I'm not sure how long we stood like that, but it felt like hours. When he finally pulled his head from me, tears were falling down his cheeks.

"We're having a baby?" He covered my stomach with both of his hands.

"Three tests said yes, so I think so." I smiled down at him as he moved to sit on the floor.

He reached for me and when I linked my hands with his, he pulled me down across from him. "We're having a baby."

"Are you happy?"

"Are you kidding, Kitten? I've wanted to knock you up since the day I met you!"

"Liar!" I laughed out loud.

"Okay, maybe not the day I met you. But pretty soon after." He reached for my face, palming it with both his hands. "I can't believe you have our baby in your belly right now. He's just in there chilling."

I rolled my eyes. "Only you would call it a *he* already. And say that it's *chilling*."

"I love you." He scooted closer to me, his lips frantic as he kissed all over my face. "I love you so much. Thank you. Thank you for loving me. Thank you for marrying me. Thank you for becoming a part of my family. And thank you for growing our love child in your belly."

"Our love child?" I snickered. "Jack Carter, you never cease to amaze me."

"You're the amazing one. I fucking love you. More than anything else in this world." He lowered his head back to my stomach and planted a kiss over my top. "And I promise I'll be a good dad."

I reached for his hand and caressed it. "I know you will."

He looked up at me and smirked. "I wasn't talking to you."

Smiling, I swatted his shoulder and said, "Well then, it knows."

"Stop calling our son an it!"

"You stop calling it a him! What if it's a girl, Jack?" My

eyes widened at the thought. "Holy shit, Jack. What if it's a girl?"

His head tipped back as he laughed full and hard. "Then I'll kill any guy who comes near her until she moves out of our house." He took a breath before continuing, "Which will be, never."

"Uh-huh," I said, knowing damn well that if we had a girl, Jack probably would go nuts every time she left the house. He reached for my hand and pressed it against his lips.

"And if we do have a girl, Kitten, I hope she looks just like her mom."

My eyes filled with tears. "Stupid pregnancy hormones. I'm going to spend nine months crying."

"Then I'll spend nine months wiping your tears."

I sniffed, wondering how in the world I'd gotten so lucky. I knew we'd been through hell and back, but all of those times felt so far rooted in the past in this present moment. We were going to have a baby, and I couldn't think of anything more amazing or wonderful.

"Kitten?" Jack's hands burrowed into his hair as he tugged at it. "You think I'll be a good dad?"

I pressed my hand against his cheek. "I know you will."

"No doubts?"

"Never," I said softly, longing with all my heart to reassure his worried mind.

"How can you be so sure?"

"Jack, I get to live every day surrounded by your love. It's deep, it's passionate, and it's intense. But it's honest and true. I know you'll love our baby the same way. No matter what sex it is."

"Damn straight!" he proclaimed, rubbing my belly as if it were a Buddha. "There's a little Carter in there. And I'll do anything to keep you both safe, protected, and provided for. That's my job."

"See? Right there. What you just said. That's how I know." I placed my hand over his and squeezed lightly.

Jack pushed himself from the floor before reaching for my hand and pulling me up with him. He wrapped his arms around me and held me so tight, I could literally feel the love radiating between us. With a firm grip on my hand, Jack pulled me toward the bed and sat down before making room for me between his legs. I sat on the bed in front of him and settled in, feeling the muscles of his chest press against my back as he spoke.

"When are you planning on moving, Kitten? I can't have you all the way across the country. I'll go fucking crazy knowing you're alone. I need you with me." He planted soft kisses along my neck and shoulders.

"I know. I'll hire movers as soon as I get back."

"What about your work? Does Nora know you're leaving?"

I turned my body to glance at him. "Shit! I forgot to tell you. Nora told me I could work on an assignment basis. I had to give her a resignation letter and everything."

"So, what does that mean? Do you still get to do the shoot with Matteo and Trina after the baby's born?"

"Yes, I just have to fly back to New York to do it. And whenever an assignment comes up that I'm qualified for and interested in, I just accept the offer. But I don't have to accept anything, or I can accept everything." I shrugged my shoulders. "Now that I'm pregnant, though, I'm not sure what I want to do."

"What do you mean, Kitten? You want to stay home with our son?"

"Jack, stop!" I giggled and rolled my eyes even though he couldn't see, then turned my body around to face him. "But I think I do. Want to stay home, that is. Plus, I really want to be there for you and travel together as much as possible."

Looking deep into his eyes, wanting to be sure he saw the sincerity in mine, I said, "You see, I had this epiphany on the train home the other day. You're my home. I don't want to be where you're not. And I know those feelings are only going to magnify once the baby comes. I'll want to keep our family together as often as possible. So, if my career sits on the back burner for now, I'm totally okay with that."

Jack held a hand in the air to stop me. "Are you sure? You're okay with not working? I know how much you love photography, and I don't want you to resent me or hate me somewhere down the line. I'm in this for the long haul, Kitten. I'm not planning on ever letting you go, so I can't have you hating me in five years."

"I want to do this. It's my choice. I want my family to come first, and you," I choked back a sob, "you're my family. I'm not saying I'll never work again, I just don't want to work for now. Priorities, babe. These are my new ones."

Jack sighed. "God, Kitten, I want to fight you on this right now. I want to tell you that you're wrong and stupid and should never quit working because you love it so much, but I'm too busy feeling so happy with everything you just said. Not because you're giving up something you love, but because there's no one else on earth I'd rather have raise our son than you. And if that means I get to spend more time with you at home, on the road, wherever—I'm thrilled."

Then he cupped my cheek with his hand, looked deep into my eyes, and said, "Every moment with you is never enough; I always want more. And I always will."

Hearing that, I broke out into tears again.

Fucking hormones.

Moving Home

Cassie

One Month Later ...

The following week, I'd hired movers to pack and move our apartment. Saying good-bye to not only the view, but the city and our friends, was extremely hard. I knew we'd keep in touch, but the reality was that it wasn't the same once you didn't get to see one another whenever you wanted.

Plus, I had fallen in love with New York City. It was harder to leave than I anticipated. I mourned the loss of my second home, a city that was so opposite from where I was from, but filled my heart in much the same way. Tears were shed, and not because I was pregnant.

Well, maybe a little.

The movers drove all of our belongings to a storage unit near Gran and Gramps' place, where we all took turns stacking boxes into the rented space. Except Jack had everyone on strict orders that I wasn't to move or carry much of anything, unless it was super light. So I ended up spending the majority of the day watching them do all the work. I felt like an ass.

Since Jack was already staying in his old bedroom at Gran's, I joined him there until I could find us a house to live in. It was hard looking for a place while I traveled with Jack and attended all his home games at a new stadium.

I had to learn new faces, meet new wives and girlfriends, remember what it was like to drive in LA traffic again, all while battling morning sickness that usually turned into afternoon sickness, followed by night sickness. Aside from that, everything was great. When I told Jack that I needed to stay back from the team's last road trip to look at houses, he begrudgingly agreed.

Jack claimed to understand, but said he didn't like it. The only way he'd accept my staying away from him was if I finally found us a home to live in. As much as we loved Gran and Gramps, we desperately needed our own space. And with the baseball season coming to a close, I wanted to find one soon. We had such a limited amount of time before the season started back up again, that I longed to be as comfortable as possible as soon as I could. Plus with the baby coming, I needed to be settled.

What could I say? I'd always been a planner.

Jack hated not being near me while I was pregnant and had insisted I come with him on every road trip. He made sure I was catered to constantly, with whatever I was craving at the moment waiting for me when I checked into our hotel room, along with extra pillows, crackers, and a mini fridge chock-full of ginger ale.

Truth be told, I loved the way Jack doted over me and protected me. I felt safe with him; I always had. My thoughts drifted back to the night of the mugging when we were still in college. I remembered how scared I was, my body filled with shock, confusion, and sadness at everything that had transpired that evening. The emotion that impressed itself on me the most was the feeling that took over my entire being the moment I saw Jack. When he pulled me into his arms, I knew everything was going to be okay because he was there. I had relaxed instantly, allowing Jack to do what Jack does best: protect what's his.

I loved traveling with him, but I was exhausted. And begging off that last road trip was worth it. So worth it. Because ... I found this house.

Oh God, this house.

Swoon.

I felt lucky enough being able to move back home knowing that all our family would be here when the baby was born, but the house we just bought was another blessing altogether. The one thing we had missed the most while we lived in New York was the SoCal beaches. There were plenty of beaches in New York, but it wasn't the same.

Hanging out with friends, surfing, and bonfires were part of growing up in Southern California. Not to mention the fact that the Pacific Ocean was one of my earliest photography obsessions. Looking for a place close to the baseball stadium, our families, and with a good school district for the baby, the Newport Beach area seemed like the best answer. Not to mention the fact I'd have daily photographic inspiration to keep my soul satisfied.

The price tag deterred me initially. I made great money in my job at the magazine, and Jack's baseball contract was more than most people would ever make in a lifetime, but I still liked to be smart when it came to our finances. And dropping millions of dollars on a house scared the ever-living shit out of me. Plus, Jack could get traded again at any time and then what? We'd have a crazy-expensive house that we never lived in?

But then Jack reminded me that we'd always want our home base to be in Southern California. Even if he did get traded again, we should still have a house where we wanted to end up in the long run. And he was right. So after weeks of home shopping without Jack, I found the perfect one in a gated community, which I knew Jack would love.

The house was two stories with four bedrooms, an office, and a gorgeous backyard with a swimming pool and a lush lawn. The master bedroom had a wraparound balcony and the moment I saw it, I instantly longed for a telescope. I'd asked my dad for one as a kid, but like many others, that promise never materialized. The tipping point was the house had a view to die for—you could see the ocean from every room in the house. When I walked through the front door for the first time and saw the ocean view from the windows, I was stunned. And sold.

Jack's eyes lit up when I brought him to the property. Luckily, the previous owners had modernized the home, so there was nothing I wanted to change, not a single thing. And the best part was that the owners desperately wanted to get rid of it, so we got it for a "steal."

On moving day, I watched as Jack wiped his brow, sweat dripping from him in beads. He and Dean stacked boxes from the moving truck we'd rented into various rooms in the new house while I worked on unpacking and setting things up. I wanted our house to look like home as soon as possible, so while they unloaded, I unpacked.

I was amazed at everything we accomplished this way. The truck that just hours prior had been filled to the gills, was now almost empty. And the walls of our home that were bare a few hours before, were now filled with artwork and framed photographs. It was as if we'd lived here for years.

"Kitten, you don't have to do that. I can hire someone," Jack shouted from the garage.

"Stop being crazy. I'm perfectly capable of hanging artwork and unpacking our stuff."

Jack sauntered into the house and grabbed me by the backside, then spun me around. "I worry about you," he said before leaning over to plant a kiss on my barely-there tummy. "Don't we?" he told my belly in a high-pitched silly voice. "We worry about Mommy. She needs to just sit down and look pretty while we do all the work."

I burst out laughing and ruffled his hair. "You're an idiot."

He looked up with a grin. "Yeah. But I'm your idiot." Jack kissed my stomach again before walking into the kitchen. He opened the fridge, reached in, and tossed Dean a beer. "Heads up," he shouted as Dean jumped and moved to catch it.

"Dick." Dean popped open the can and took a long gulp. And then almost spit it right back out at the sound of my best friend's voice.

"Ah, I can't believe you guys are back here! I'm so happy." Melissa bounced into the house and straight into my arms. She glanced at Dean and Jack, giving them a curt smile before pressing her ear against my stomach. "How's my little baby?"

she cooed, then rubbed my belly like it was a fucking good luck charm.

Why does everyone do this?

Jack and Dean scuttled out the sliding glass door to the backyard. The cowards.

When they'd left, I folded my arms over my chest and said flatly, "Still not talking to Dean, I see?"

She tilted her head to one side. "*He's* not talking to me, not the other way around."

I frowned. "You broke his heart. What do you expect?"

"I expect you, of all people, not to take sides."

"How can I take sides?" I said with a huff. "You never even tried."

Melissa's face fell as tears filled her eyes. "That was harsh."

"I don't understand you. At all. You're the one who told me to fight for Jack, to not give up on him. You pushed me to love him and give him a chance," I pointed out, then took a deep breath in and out to fight the nausea I felt growing. "More than once."

"So?" she snapped.

"Soooo," I said pointedly. "You never follow your own advice."

"How do you even know I want to?"

"Because I can see it in your eyes. You miss him. And there's something you're not telling me. Come on." I grabbed her hand and yanked her toward the garage.

"Where are we going?" She tried to tug her hand away, and I only pulled her harder.

"Get in the car." I opened the passenger door and shoved

her inside. "I'm sick of this and we're going to the only place where you'll listen to reason."

"Oh my God. No." She pressed the button to unlock the door and I hit it again, just as fast, using the child safety locks to trap her in the car. "You cannot Gran-ify me!" she screamed out, pounding on the side window.

"Stop beating up my car! And seriously? Gran-ify you?"

"Yeah!" she cried out. "Where you bring me to Gran and Gramps and they say the most perfect things and I leave there in tears because you were right all along and I was an idiot."

I wanted to laugh, oh so badly, but stopped myself. "Let's just see what they have to say. Maybe they won't be on my side?" I offered, silently knowing that they would.

I mean, I hoped they would. They'd better.

"So you're saying they're actually neutral? Ha! I'll believe that when I hear it."

A few minutes later I pulled into their driveway, hoping they wouldn't be upset at our unannounced arrival. Giving a quick knock, I didn't wait for a response before opening the front door and shouting, "Gran? Gramps?"

"Cassie? Is that you, dear?" Gran shouted from the kitchen.

Of course. They're always in the kitchen.

"Is that our Kitten?" Gramps called out and I stifled a laugh.

We walked through the entryway, Melissa's hand firmly in mine as I pulled her through. "Sit," I demanded and she did as I asked, but folded her arms over her chest and put on that stubborn face I know so well.

"Oh! Hi, Melissa." Gran smiled. "Are you two okay? What's going on? Is the baby all right?" She eyed my belly and

I nodded.

"Everything's good, Gran. I just needed to bring Melissa here."

Gran's brow furrowed, but I knew it was part of her act. "Whatever for, dear?"

"Because for some reason she won't date Dean. And I know it isn't because she doesn't like him, or miss him, or any normal reason. I figured that only you and Gramps could get to the bottom of this. So, go on. Work your magic. Use your granny voodoo on her."

Gran and Gramps laughed, full-out belly laughs. "Granny voodoo. That's great, Kitten," Gramps said between fits of laughter.

"I'm not kidding! She's broken," I shouted, pointing at my now terrified best friend. "Fix her!"

"Well, I will admit that I'm not sure why it's taken this long for the two of you kids to get together," Gran began. "Why don't you tell me what the problem is, Melissa?"

Melissa inhaled deeply, her gaze shifting between the three of us all staring at her. "There is no problem. Maybe that's the problem?"

"What?" Gramps scratched his head, completely taken aback by her answer.

"Go on," Gran prompted, her tone sympathetic. It's how she always sucks them in.

"That's it. There's no problem," Melissa said, obviously trying to sound confident.

"Do you like Dean?" I asked the most obvious question of them all and watched as her face softened the way it had when she first mentioned him back in the student union when we were in college.

All eyes fixed on Melissa, waiting for her answer. She looked down and wiped at her eyes. "Of course I like him. I've never liked anyone so much before."

I stood there, shocked. This made absolutely no sense at all to me. I shook my head and said, "Seriously? Then what the hell are we doing here? Why aren't you with him?"

Gran huffed out a breath before pulling a bottle of wine from the cupboard. Opening the bottle, she poured three glasses, then filled a fourth with cold water. "Sorry to drink in front of you, dear," she said in apology, handing me the glass filled with water.

"It's okay. Wine doesn't sound good anyway." I patted my stomach.

She placed one of the glasses in front of Melissa. "Drink. Let's discuss this."

"You girls make everything so complicated. Don't you know us men are simple folk?" Gramps asked as he sipped his wine.

Gran held a hand in the air to stop him, then asked Melissa, "You're scared, aren't you, dear?"

Gramps nodded. "It's so obvious."

My head swiveled back and forth as Melissa's tears fell. "What is? What's obvious?" I asked, completely confused.

"She's afraid it won't work. That they won't last," Gran said softly as she watched Melissa.

Gramps smacked the kitchen counter with his hand. "Kitten,

what's wrong with your girl?"

"She's just scared. That's all this is. Pure fear," Gran said.

"Seriously?" I asked Melissa. "But you're like the most fearless person I know. You're always telling people what they should be doing. Always encouraging and always telling them to take risks."

"It's easy to tell other people what to do," she admitted. "It's a lot harder to apply your advice to your own life, especially when you don't see it as clearly."

"What the hell are you talking about?" I asked.

Melissa sighed. "I knew that you and Jack were meant to be together. I could see it, you know? I always told you that. So it's easy for me to push you to go for something that's so obvious to me and everyone else around you. But I don't see myself or my situation with the same kind of clarity."

"Really?" I said with a snort. "Why don't I believe you?"

She nodded. "It's true. I can tell you what I think you should do, but I never know what I should."

"Well, we all know what you should do! You should do Dean! Um ..." I stopped, feeling the heat on my cheeks rise. "I mean, we all know you and Dean belong together, so what aren't you telling me? Spit it out," I insisted.

Melissa sucked in a deep breath and blurted out, "Fine! I like Dean. I really do. But if something happens between us and we don't work out, I'm the one who loses, not him. You're *my* best friend," she reminded me, glancing in my direction. "But *he's* your husband's brother. If we hook up and it ends badly, one of us loses you guys."

Her eyes pleaded with me for understanding. "And it sure as

shit isn't going to be Dean. I'm pretty sure he can't stop being Jack's brother. But I can stop being your best friend." Tears spilled freely down her face, and she reached up to swipe them away. "I don't want to stop being your best friend. I don't want to be the one who loses everything."

My heart aching for her, I stood up and walked over to Melissa, then wrapped my arms around her and squeezed. "I'll never stop being your best friend. No matter what happens between you and Dean."

She shook her head. "You say that now, but you don't know that. You can't be sure, if you had to choose. I mean, if you were forced to choose. There's no way you could choose me over Dean. He's family now."

"But you've always been my family, too." I caught Melissa's gaze, trying to show her how sincere I was, but she shook her head.

Gramps added, "I can guarantee you that Dean isn't thinking about everything he's going to lose if you guys break up. He probably isn't thinking that you guys will break up at all. Why are you?"

"Yes, hon, why are you so convinced that you two won't last?" Gran added.

"Seriously, Melissa, you're the one person in the world who pushed for me to not give up on Jack. Even after everything we went through, you still said he was the one for me."

"Well, he was. I was right," she snapped.

"And so am I. You and Dean are meant to be together too. You're the only one who doesn't see it."

Her head lowered as she whispered, "I feel it."

"Listen, Melissa." Gran reached over and took my friend's hand in hers. "Love is the one thing in this world worth taking a risk for. When you're older and you look back on the life you lived, you won't regret the fact that you took the chance to love someone. But you will regret the chances on love you didn't take. Especially the ones rooted in fear. They're only scary because you have the most to lose. You feel the most for them. Don't let the fear of losing love stop you from having the experience altogether."

"She's right, you know." Gramps smiled warmly. "She usually is, though, so that's not surprising. But if you walk away, you will regret this, darlin'. Maybe not right now or not a few years down the road. But eventually you will regret this moment. And every other moment you had with our grandson that could have led to more. Life is filled with many things. You don't want regrets to be one of them."

Gran stood up and planted a sloppy kiss on Gramps' cheek, and he slipped his arm around her. "He has a point, dear. Live without regrets. It's very easy to, really. You just listen to your heart, follow it, and take chances. Always take chances. And take risks, especially when it comes to love. Because love is the one thing in this world that's worth risking everything for."

Melissa nodded, her expression more relaxed and open, her stubborn face a thing of the past. The conversation had been simple, but effective.

After thanking Gran and Gramps and promising to bring them to the new house soon, I practically sprinted to the car. I wanted to fly back to the house. Getting Melissa there so she could work this bullshit out with Dean was my number one priority. I couldn't wait for them to finally be together. We made it home in record time while I kept conversation to a minimum, not daring to mess up the magic that Gran and Gramps had worked on Melissa.

I pulled the car into the driveway a little too fast, and pulled the emergency brake before hopping out.

Jack walked into the garage as Melissa got out of the car. "Where'd you two run off to?"

"We had some business to take care of. Where's Dean?" I asked.

"He left. He has a date tonight or some such shit," he said, looking at Melissa as he said the damning words.

Melissa caved in on herself then; she almost crumbled. If a person could break into little pieces and fall to the ground like glass, I knew I was about to witness it.

"He has a date?" I shouted. "With who? Call him! Stop him!"

"What's going on? Where have you guys been?" Jack narrowed his eyes.

I placed a hand on my hip, and said pointedly, "I took her to see Gran and Gramps. We needed to talk it out."

"So, did you? Talk it out, I mean?" Jack's gaze drifted to Melissa, and his eyes widened a little as he noticed her bloodshot eyes and reddened nose.

"She did," I answered for her. "But we need Dean here. Right now. He can't go on a date without hearing this first. He has to know!"

I was losing it. My control, my patience, all of it. If Dean went on this date and we allowed Melissa to sleep on everything she'd learned today, she might wake up tomorrow and decide not to ever tell him. And all this progress would be for nothing. I needed these two to finally get together. Not only because she was my best friend and he was my brother-in-law, but because they were well suited for each other and we all knew it. I wanted more than anything for them to at least try.

"So you want me to call my brother?" Jack asked, his voice filled with confusion. "And tell him to cancel his date and come back over here? Am I getting this right?"

"Forget it!" I said with frustration. "I'll call him myself." I reached for my phone, pressed Dean's name, and hit the CALL button.

Nerves shot through me as I pushed Melissa into the house and pointed at the vodka. Jack shrugged his shoulders and I rolled my eyes. I grabbed a shot glass from the cabinet as Dean picked up. Slamming the glass on the granite countertop, I glared at Jack as I pointed at the vodka and then at my trembling best friend.

"Dean, hey! Thank you so much for all your help today, but you left something here. Can you come back and get it?" I had no idea why I lied, but it seemed right at the time.

"What did I leave there? I didn't bring anything."

I scrambled, waving my hands in the air silently begging for help, but no one moved or made a sound. "I, uh, had a gift for you. But it will go bad if you don't come get it." My face twisted with each lie that spilled from my mouth.

"Sis, I'm getting ready to pick up a date. I'll be late if I come by there."

"Listen to me right now, Dean. I'm pregnant, emotional,

and out of control. If you do not get over here in the next ten minutes," I paused for half a second to think it through before clarifying, "*without* your date, I will hang you by your balls the next time I see you. Understood?"

"Fine. I'm on my way."

I ended the call without saying another word. Glancing at Melissa, I noticed the empty shot glass and smiled. "Good girl. A little liquid courage never hurts."

"Shit, Cass," Melissa breathed out on a moan. "What am I gonna say to him?"

Jack cleared his throat. "Is anyone going to tell me what the hell is going on?"

"You'll see," I said with a smirk toward Jack before looking into Melissa's bright blue eyes. "And as for you. You will tell him everything we talked about at Gran and Gramps'. Just be honest."

Pouring myself a glass of water, I sat on one of our new barstools and waited for the sound of Dean's Mustang to pull into the driveway. If it felt like forever to me, I could only imagine how Melissa must have felt.

The rumble of his engine alerted us to his arrival. I opened the large garage door as Dean rushed through it and into the house through another connecting door. I closed the large garage door behind him and stepped back into the kitchen where we had all gathered. His eyes scanned quickly over the three of us, all but skipping Melissa's face.

"Okay, I'm here," he huffed out, the smell of his cologne filling the kitchen area as I silently thanked the pregnancy gods for not making it nauseate me. Dean looked hot in his dark blue jeans. He had on a fitted black T-shirt underneath a dark blue and black button-down shirt that wasn't buttoned. "Is anyone going to tell me what's going on?"

I waited for Melissa to speak up, move, or do something. Her fingers tapped out a noiseless tune on the rim of her glass as she stared at the floor and refused to look up.

Tired of waiting, I snapped my fingers in front of her face, forcing her to acknowledge me. When her broken eyes met mine, I wanted to take her into my arms and comfort her. She opened and closed her mouth a couple of times, as if she wanted to say something, but no words came out.

You've got to be kidding me.

Never in all the years I'd known Melissa had I ever seen her like this before, and I wondered if it were a side of her she'd always kept to herself. She'd obviously clammed up, so I guessed it was up to me to poke her with a sharp stick.

"I called you back here, Dean, because I thought Melissa had something to tell you. But I guess I was wrong." It was a little harsh and I knew it, but game time was over and I only wanted to help.

Dean's gaze snapped to Melissa and I saw what looked like hope flash in his eyes. He raised his eyebrows in her direction, but neither spoke a word.

I glanced at Jack, who had leaned against the wall, his arms folded and his feet crossed at the ankle. He kept his mouth shut and pinged his gaze between Dean and Melissa, clearly fascinated by what was unfolding. I had to laugh a little to myself, thinking that he was probably partially thankful that the drama had nothing to do with us for once.

Dean nodded slowly, and said to Melissa, "So, is that true? Do you have something to tell me, or are we just going to stand here all night? Because if it's the latter, then I have a date to go apologize to."

Melissa's face paled and tightened as her stubborn defensive nature took over. She narrowed her reddened eyes and snapped, "Go then. You shouldn't keep her waiting."

"Are you fucking kidding me?" Dean shouted. "Is this a joke? Goddammit, woman, if you have something to say to me, just say it already!"

She stomped across the kitchen to stop in front of Dean and glare up at him, her tiny frame dwarfed by his. Then Melissa grabbed his shirtsleeve and dragged him out of the kitchen and into the garage without shutting the door.

Knowing I should grab Jack and walk away to give the couple their privacy, I planted my feet on the kitchen floor and leaned toward the open door instead. Eavesdropping might have been a crappy thing to do, but I had a lot invested in this conversation and was dying to hear it.

My husband obviously felt the same, because he wrapped his arm around me and pulled me against his body as he leaned toward the garage as well. "I'm not moving, so don't even ask. I want to hear this shit," he whispered against my ear.

I turned my head and planted a kiss on his soft lips. That single peck fanned the embers of lust inside me, causing them to erupt. Instantly, I wanted to drag him to the bedroom and christen it right the fuck now, but I shook my head to douse the flames, and concentrated on what was happening in the garage.

"So, what is this big news you have to tell me?" Dean

attempted to sound tough, but I knew he had to be dying inside.

"I need you to stop being so mean right now," Melissa begged. "Please? This is really hard for me."

I wished I could see Dean's face. Or at least his hazel eyes. I imagined them instantly softening with her words.

"I'll stop," he replied.

"Thanks." She sucked in a long breath before letting it out slowly. "First, I just want you to know that I do like you, Dean. I always have."

"You like me, like me?" he interrupted, his tone surprised, and I had to stop myself from giggling at his word choice.

"So much," she said, then paused as it sounded like she was pacing across our garage floor.

Jack poked me in the shoulder, his eyes wide with excited shock. I nodded with a tight-lipped grin as Melissa continued, "And I'm so sorry for everything. The way I acted and pretending like I didn't care."

"Why? Why did you pretend? You fucking crushed me in New York. Why would you do that?" Dean's voice was pained as he referred to their trip to visit us several months before.

"I just got scared," she said in a small voice.

"Of what?"

Silence.

I squeezed Jack's arm as I waited for her response. Pressing my lips against his face, I whispered into Jack's ear, "This is killing me."

"Me too," he admitted.

Minutes of continued silence passed, deafening us all with the possibilities not yet spoken.

"Melissa," Dean said, his voice finally breaking through the quiet. "Scared of what? You have to tell me. Please. Don't close off now."

Footsteps shuffled outside our line of vision and I held my breath.

"Please. I want to know," Dean pleaded.

"You're Jack's brother and I'm Cassie's best friend. We're going to be in each other's lives forever. I was afraid that if we tried to be together and it didn't work out, it would ruin everything. That everything would be awkward and uncomfortable. And one of us would eventually have to leave, and well, it's not going to be you, because you're freaking related to Jack. So it would be me. I'd get kicked out of the group because you and I tried to love each other and it didn't work out. So then I wouldn't have only lost you, but my best friend and her baby too."

Jack caught my eye and whispered angrily, "What am I, chopped liver? She'd lose me too!"

Shaking my head at his narcissistic view of the world, I shot an elbow into his ribs to shut him up.

Back in the garage, Dean laughed. "Is that it?" he said to tease Melissa, and I couldn't stop the small laugh that escaped my lips.

"What do you mean, is that it? That's everything, Dean. Cassie's my best friend. Do you know how important that is to a girl? I can't lose her. I can't lose you both."

The sound of my best friend crying pained me. Jack knew I wanted to go in there and comfort her, so he tightened his grip on my body. "Let them work this out," he reminded me with a soft kiss to the back of my head.

Dean's voice was soothing as he said, "I know how important your friendship is to both of you. I'd never come between you. You know I'd never want that." When he finished, more shuffling sounds filtered through the open door.

"Of course you wouldn't want it, but that doesn't mean it won't happen. Even by just talking about this, we're opening up something we can't take back."

"I don't want to take it back," he said in a low voice.

"You say that now." Melissa sniffed, sounding so pitiful my heart broke a little more for her.

"I'll say that always. I want to be with you. I've always wanted to be with you. Why are you so convinced we won't last?"

"I'm not convinced," she replied. "I'm just worried. I'm a planner. Us not working out can't be part of the plan because it ruins the rest of my plans."

Jack gave me a questioning look and I shrugged. I honestly had no idea what plans she referred to.

Dean laughed and Melissa sobbed a little louder, then whined, "Don't laugh at me."

"I'm not laughing at you. I'm in love with you."

"You're," she paused, her voice catching, "in love with me? Even after everything?"

"I knew you'd eventually come around," he said confidently. "I just got really tired of waiting and getting shot down."

"You knew?"

"Well, I hoped. I hoped a lot," he admitted and I smiled at

the sound of it. "So, can we do this now? You and me? Can we make this happen?"

"Are you sure you want to?"

"How many times do I have to tell you the same thing? I want this. I want this now. I'll want this tomorrow. I'll want this forever."

"You don't know that," she said softly. "You can't be sure."

Dean sighed. "Melissa, I'm so convinced we'll last until we die, that I'd bet money on it."

"Oh yeah? What kind of money?" she asked in such a normal voice that I couldn't stop my laughter from bursting free. "Hey!" she called out to us. "I hear you in there. Eavesdroppers."

"Takes one to know one!" I shouted in response before hearing the familiar sounds of kissing.

I smacked Jack's shoulder again and pulled from his grip to creep toward the door that separated the kitchen from the garage. Peeking around the door, the sight I saw made me cover my face with my hands. The sight of them actually kissing in public, well, at least in front of other people, was bizarre after the history they've had.

I resisted the temptation to light off fireworks, or hire a band. We'd all waited so long for this to happen, I wanted the whole world to know it finally had. When I turned to walk back to Jack, neither one of us could stop grinning. He opened his arms and I fell into them, kissing each dimple once before finding his mouth.

"I am so happy for them! My God, can you believe it?"

His tongue teased my bottom lip before begging for entry

into my mouth. I complied, letting the beer-flavored taste of him consume me.

"Jeez, you two, get a room," Melissa teased, and I pulled away from my husband to see her wrapped in Dean's arms.

I gave a little huff. "You're one to talk. You two need the room. You have a lot of make-up sex to have," I teased as Dean perked up.

"I like that idea. I think she's right." Dean looked down at my fun-sized best friend and kissed her.

"Don't you have a date to get to?" Jack asked pointedly, like a smartass.

Dean winced. "I think I'm late."

"Tell me you at least canceled and the poor girl isn't sitting at home wondering where you are?" I pinned him with the "mom" look I've been practicing lately in the mirror, and he chuckled.

"Who do you think I am? Jack?"

Melissa shook her head, then sucked in a breath before admitting, "I hope you're done dating other people."

"I hope you're done dating anyone. Ever. 'Cause it's never happening for you again."

"Is that so?" she fired back, my little spitfire reemerging, which made me very happy. A meek and broken Melissa was so not the girl I knew and loved.

"Deny it all you want," Dean told her. "Be scared all you want. I'll be here to remind you. This is the real deal right here. Me and you?" he said, drawing a finger between the two of them. "This is gonna last."

"So this is really happening? The two of you are finally a

flipping couple! Am I dreaming?" I walked over to Melissa and hugged her before doing the same to Dean.

"You're not, but I think I am," Melissa said dryly.

Jack opened the fridge and pulled out two beers. "Time to man up. Drink," he said, tossing a can at Dean. "Fun-Size, you need another shot of liquid courage? Not that it helped."

Dean looked down at her, a playful smile on his face. "You did shots before I got here?"

"Correction, I did a shot. One. And yeah. I thought I was going to throw up on your shoes if I didn't."

He wiggled his right foot. "I like these shoes."

I hopped up on the counter, my legs and feet dangling over the side. "Hey, I have a question."

Melissa's perfect little eyebrows drew together as she asked, "What is it?"

"While Jack was eavesdropping on you guys, and I couldn't help but overhear because I refuse to leave his side," I said innocently as Jack poked me in the ribs. "What did you mean about all your plans? Or the rest of your plans or something?"

She pressed her lips together before blurting out, "It's all wrapped up in the same thing. The breakup. I lose him first," she said, pointing at Dean before continuing. "Then I lose my best friend. And then I lose her kids. And so that means that I don't get to have kids with you and our kids won't be best friends and we won't move next door to each other or raise our babies together or do any of the things that I completely plan on doing with you. Because that's what best friends do. We have kids together and shop together and our families grow up together."

I tried to kick her, but my foot wouldn't reach that far and I refused to hop down from the counter. "You're a dork. Just marry Dean and then we can do all those things, 'kay?"

Dean looked down at Melissa and squeezed her shoulders. "Yeah, just marry me. Problem solved."

"I'm serious!" she practically screamed.

"So am I!" Dean yelled back.

"Enough!" Jack pressed his hands around each side of my stomach as if the baby's ears were there. "You're going to stress out my baby. And I'll fucking kill both of you if you do that. Don't shout around my kid," he said forcefully, and I rolled my eyes. "If our baby comes out rolling his eyes, Kitten, so help me God—"

"Yeah? So help you God, what? What are you going to do?" I shot back playfully.

Jack slammed his fist against the granite. "I don't know, but I'll think of something to torture you with!"

"You two are ridiculous," Melissa said as she snuggled closer into Dean's arms.

I stuck my tongue out at her and she did the same. "You," I pointed at her, "are not ever allowed to say that to anyone. Ever. You're the most ridiculous couple I've ever met."

"You gonna let her talk to us like that, Melis?" Dean taunted.

Melissa narrowed her eyes playfully. "You want me to hit a pregnant chick?" She made a fist and punched her other hand with it.

Jack stepped into the space separating us. "I will hurt you, Fun-Size. No one messes with my baby mama."

"Oh my gosh, how long have you been waiting to use that line?" I doubled over laughing, along with everyone else.

"Weeks," he admitted with a dimpled smile before stepping between my legs.

I love those dimples.

I hope our baby has those dimples.

"I almost forgot, I have something for you." Jack perked up and disappeared into the garage. I heard one of the car doors open and close, then Jack walked back into the kitchen.

He tossed a small package at me and I caught it with both hands. "What in the world?"

"Just open it."

I peeled back the wrapping paper to reveal a small cardboard box. When I opened the top and looked inside, I gasped with surprise, then pulled out a miniature mason jar filled with quarters.

Jack beamed at me. "Those are for all the belly touches. I'm going to be touching your belly a lot. I figured I oughta pay up."

Shaking my head in amazement, I glanced around the room at some of the various jars proudly displayed, each jar filled to be brim with quarters, and representing different times in our lives. The original jar he gave me in college sat in our bedroom, untouched.

I'd taken the jars of quarters from when he asked to be traded to the Mets and placed them in my new home office. They reminded me of everything he sacrificed to win me back, and looking at them made me happy. There were other various-sized jars from throughout our years in New York, when we refused to spend them. We collected every quarter that came into our possession. And now we'd be starting our California collection. I knew right where this miniature mason jar would be displayed: our baby's room.

"I think you still have a few touches left from the other quarters," I reminded him, waving my arm in the direction of one of the jars in the living room.

"You can never be too safe. Can you, baby?" He pressed his lips against my stomach and I rubbed the top of his head, feeling more content than ever.

Happy Birthday

Cassie

Jack and I finished moving into our Newport Beach house without any issues, and I found myself stunned every morning when I opened my eyes and could see the ocean from our bedroom window. The beauty floored me and I prayed I'd never get used to it or take it for granted.

Matteo and Trina had their baby girl in November. They named her Adalynn, and I flew to New York in January to photograph them for the magazine. The pictures turned out stunning, but it didn't hurt when all three of your subjects were gorgeous. They were set to be the featured article online, as well as in print in one of the summer issues.

Trina was thrilled to see me and my growing belly, and she couldn't wait to give me all sorts of tips and tricks to stay comfortable and fit during the pregnancy. She was obsessed with pillows and told me I needed at least eight. Who needed eight pillows to sleep? I laughed, but she made me promise to buy more.

She also talked about maternity yoga and prenatal massages, and basically refused to acknowledge the fact that I wasn't a freaking supermodel before the baby and I sure as hell wasn't going to be one after. But I missed her. And I made her promise she'd come visit.

Matteo squeezed me and rubbed my belly when he saw me at the airport. He was happy to see me, but he admitted he wished that Jack could have come too. It was too close to spring training for the pitchers and catchers, so Jack stayed behind to pack and get ready. "It's like old times," Matteo said while driving me to their apartment, and I almost started crying. It felt amazing to be in the city, but so much had changed in such a short amount of time.

As hard as it had been to leave, I knew without a doubt that I didn't belong there anymore. At least, not right now. Plus, I couldn't see raising a kid in Manhattan. Being in the city as an adult felt like one thing, but raising a child in a city that busy and bustling seemed like another. I supposed when it came down to it, I was a California girl through and through. I liked the suburbs, with their front and back yards, and neighbors you actually came to know.

I walked through the sea of red-clad Angel fans, my stomach protruding like I was smuggling in a beach ball under my maternity top. Silently, I cursed Jack, wishing that I had been smart enough to time my pregnancy with an off-season due date. But then again, we hadn't really planned it anyway.

Making my way into the players' wives section, I smiled at

my new companions and forced my growing body into the tiny green stadium seat. I looked down the aisle at Ashley, the ridiculously cute blonde wife of one of the veterans. She was the queen bee of the wives on this team, their Kymber, but minus the horrible attitude. Every team probably had their own Kymber, but I never wanted to be her. At least Ashley hadn't treated me badly when I first arrived. I wasn't sure if it was because Jack had already paid his dues in the organization, or if it was because we were married and I didn't work, but I didn't care. Whatever created less drama and stress in my everyday life was good enough for me.

"How are you feeling, Cassie?" Ashley smiled from behind her oversized sunglasses.

I rested my hands on top of my huge belly. "Like a whale," I huffed out. This kid was heavy. My lower back hurt and my ankles were swollen. Not like I could see my ankles anymore, but I could feel them.

How come no one ever warned you that one day you'd look down for your feet and they'd be gone? One day out of the blue, my feet disappeared beneath the oversized growth in my stomach and I freaked out. No matter how hard I tried to see them, I couldn't. It was scary to lose your feet. I decided right then and there that the next time someone I knew got pregnant, I would warn them, *One day you'll wake up and your feet will be gone. Do you need a pedicure? Are your feet dry? Who knows, because you can't see them.*

The freakiness of losing my feet was one thing, but losing the private part of me was another. That had disappeared earlier, but it was still traumatic. Jack laughed at me when I told him I had no idea what was going on down there. He promised to keep an eye on it for me. How comforting.

The sound of someone shuffling to the seat next to me stopped me from feeling sorry for myself. I turned to see a girl I didn't recognize. The poor thing, she looked terrified.

"Hi," she said softly, her long brown hair falling in front of her brown eyes as she directed her gaze toward the field in front of us.

"Hi. You must be new." I hesitated, wondering if this girl was actually the girlfriend of someone on the team, or just a weekend fling. I'd seen enough girls come and go over the years that I finally understood why the other wives tended to keep their distance, but it still didn't explain the outright nastiness once they knew the girl belonged to one of the players. There was no acceptable reason for that kind of behavior.

She nodded. "My boyfriend just got called up from the Salt Lake City team."

"What position does he play?" I hoped he wasn't a pitcher. Don't ask me why, since I knew the team's roster carried more pitchers than any other position on the team. I think it boiled down to my being scared for Jack. The whole thing with the Mets had scarred me. I'd learned the hard way how disposable and replaceable the players were once they no longer fit the team's long-term goals.

"He's a catcher," she said, and I recognized the pride beaming in her eyes.

"How long have you guys been dating?" I asked. She looked so young. A lot younger than I knew I looked when Jack was called up.

"A few years. We're high school sweethearts." A breath escaped as she glanced down at my belly. "And you? Who's your husband?"

"Oh, I'm Cassie," I answered, extending my hand toward hers. She grabbed it for a firm shake. "Jack Carter's my husband. And he did this to me." I looked down at my monstrosity with chagrin as she giggled.

"I'm Shawna. It's nice to meet you."

"Cassie? Cassie!" Ashley's voice interrupted our conversation and I turned my sunglass-covered face toward hers.

"Yeah?"

"Why don't you come sit next to me," she said coyly, patting the empty seat to her right.

"I'm okay, thanks," I told her. "I probably won't stay the whole game." I'd stopped sitting for Jack's entire games as soon as it got too uncomfortable to stay in those chairs for almost three hours. A few times I'd snuck downstairs into the tunnels, where it was cool, to wait for Jack. Even if the weather hadn't warmed up entirely, this baby kept me plenty heated.

"Are you going to switch seats?" Shawna asked.

"Nah. I'm fine right here. A word of advice—don't take it personally if the other wives don't go out of their way to play nice at first. It's just what they do until your boyfriend has paid his dues to the team." I wanted to warn her that the other women wouldn't be as kind as I was. And since she and her boyfriend had been together since they were kids, I feared she wouldn't be strong enough to handle it.

She glanced past me at the rows of other women and

shrugged. "I've dealt with worse. The girls that tried to come on to Bryce while he was playing in the minor leagues were disgusting. They were relentless and disrespectful. At least these women aren't trying to take him away from me."

I nodded in understanding. "Oh, Shawna, you have no idea. Remind me one day to tell you our story. But not now. I'm way too tired."

She flashed a pretty smile at me. "I'll hold you to that."

During the seventh inning stretch, I stood up and walked around the stadium. My aching feet were no match for my lower back; I needed to walk it off. Heading down the stairs, I marched through the concrete hallway toward the locker room. Hoping that Jack would shower quickly and not leaving me standing out here for long, I rubbed my back and concentrated on breathing. Robert, the security guard, sat on a metal folding chair, watching me.

"Any day now, right, Mrs. Carter?" he asked as he removed his ball cap and scratched the top of his balding head.

"With any luck," I said, smiling.

He nodded. "Well, you look fantastic. Absolutely glowing."

"Thank you, Robert. That's kind of you to say." I continued to smile, but doubted his words. I knew I looked like a freaking cow, and who knew what my feet looked like since I'd lost them.

The quiet tunnel became noisy as the rest of the wives and

girlfriends started to file in around me. A moment later, Jack burst through the doors and headed right for me.

"Hello, Kitten," he purred in my ear before falling to his knees and kissing my belly. "Hello, baby." He had started doing this after every game and I loved it; we didn't care who watched.

"Did you shower? The other wives just got here."

"No need, since I didn't play today, and I know how uncomfortable you are. I don't want you sitting out here waiting for me when I can shower at home."

"Thank you," I said with relief, sincerely happy with his thoughtfulness.

"Anything for my girl. And my boy." He smiled, his dimples appearing. "How are you feeling?"

"My back hurts, but otherwise I'm okay."

He grabbed my hand in his and I waddled a step behind him. Yes, I waddled; my new form of locomotion could no longer be considered walking. Once we entered the parking lot, Jack slowed his pace before popping the trunk of our black BMW and unlocking the doors. He opened the passenger door for me and helped me inside before tossing his bag into the back of the car.

"Do you want me to stop anywhere on the way home?" he asked, referring to my frequent late-night cravings.

Lately, I'd become obsessed with a very specific kind of Popsicle. I think I started eating about ten a day. And then there was the phase where I had to have cereal for every meal.

I reached for his leg and placed my hand on his thigh. "We have a freezer full of popsicles and a pantry full of cereal. I think I'm good."

"All right then," he said before stepping on the gas.

Jack's free hand moved from holding mine to resting on my giant belly. He rubbed in slow, circular motions and the heat that radiated from his hand to my stomach soothed me. A swift kick caused Jack to pull his hand away.

"He kicked me!"

I laughed. "I know. I felt that." I glanced down and noticed the baby inside me moving parts of his body. He twisted and turned as my stomach took on odd shapes to accommodate his growing length. "I know it's supposed to be miraculous and stuff, but seeing a body part poke out of my stomach is weird. And kind of creepy. I feel like there's an alien inside me."

Jack glanced at me before turning onto the freeway. "I think it's awesome. Do you have any idea how cool it is that you get to grow a person inside you? Guys can't do that."

"No shit, they can't! Guys couldn't handle it," I teased.

He nodded and raised his eyebrows meaningfully as he said with complete seriousness, "No guy wants to birth a bowling ball out of his penis."

I muffled a giggle. "Did you just say the word penis?"

"I was trying to watch my language in front of the alien baby, okay? No guy wants to birth a bowling ball out of his dick. Better?"

"Much." I sighed, and angled my body toward his as the car raced toward home.

I must have fallen asleep on the short ride home because when I opened my eyes, Jack was carrying me up the stairs.

"Babe, you're going to break your back." Embarrassed, I

tried to wiggle out of his arms but he tightened his hold.

"Can you not try to jump out of my arms while I'm walking up the stairs? Jesus, Kitten." Once we reached the top, he gently placed me on my feet. "I didn't want to wake you."

"Thank you." I attempted to wrap my arms around him, but couldn't reach anymore. The size of my stomach had grown so large, it stopped me from getting close to anyone.

"He's cock-blocking me already," Jack said with a smirk.

"I'm sure it won't be the last time," I teased.

Jack smacked my ass and I yelped. "Go get in bed. I want you off your feet. Carter's orders."

"Yes sir." I gave him a snappy salute before disappearing into the bedroom.

I woke up with Jack's hand firmly on my side. The last few weeks I'd been sleeping fitfully, waking up every few hours to pee and adjust the plethora of pillows stacked around my body. Trina had been right about them and they were lifesavers, tucked underneath my stomach, between my legs, and behind my back.

Standing to walk to the bathroom, I felt water dripping down my leg.

Shit.

I tried to hold my bladder, but I couldn't. Shuffling into the bathroom, I sat down on the toilet and the water gushed. My heart started to race as I realized that I wasn't peeing at all—my water had just broken.

"Jack," I yelled from behind the bathroom door. I heard him rustling in the bed, but he didn't respond. "Jack?"

"Kitten? Where are you?" His voice sounded groggy.

"I'm in the bathroom, Jack. It's time. I'll be out in a second." I waited for the water to stop flowing as thoughts of *this is really happening* flooded my mind. When I walked out of the bathroom, I found Jack dressed and sitting on the bed, waiting for me.

He immediately hopped up and rushed toward me. "Are you okay? Are you sure it's time?"

"My water just broke. We should go. Can you grab the overnight bag?" At my doctor's insistence, I had a bag packed for weeks now that included some clothes for me as well as clothes to bring the baby home in.

He lifted an arm and proudly displayed the packed bag, "Already grabbed it."

"You seriously impress me," I said as a contraction tore through my insides. Bending over and grabbing at my stomach, I groaned and breathed through the pain.

Jack was instantly behind me, rubbing my back. "Kitten, are you okay?" He dropped to his knees to look up into my eyes. "You'll be okay. I promise. What can I do?"

He didn't like to see me in any kind of pain, and the hurt it caused him to be unable to help made me feel even worse. When the contraction passed, I stood up straight and nodded at him. "I'm not going to change. They'll make me get out of all this anyway." I waved a hand over my pajamas.

"You look beautiful. Let's go as soon as you're ready." He

tugged at his hair like he always does when he's nervous, pulling at it.

"I'm ready." I forced a smile to help ease his nerves.

Jack's hand found my stomach as he whispered, "Please stop hurting your mommy. Daddy can't take it and it's making him crazy." His lips found mine and he pressed the softest kiss against them. "Let's go have this baby."

He walked me to the garage and around the side of our Jeep Grand Cherokee before opening the door for me and helping me in. "Why aren't we taking the Bimmer?" I asked.

"I don't know. I like the idea of being in an SUV instead of a car right now."

When he scooted into the driver's seat, he reached for my seat belt first, fastening it around my stomach before putting on his own. I focused on my breathing, paranoid that another contraction could come at any minute.

I pulled out my phone, which I'd managed to grab on my way out the door, and typed a group text to my mom, Gran, Dean, and Melissa.

On our way to the hospital. Water broke. Text you when I get settled and know our room number.

"I can't believe this is really happening. I mean, of course I knew it would happen eventually, but it's weird." I breathed slowly in and out as Jack drove through our gated neighborhood.

"How so?" he asked, resting a hand on my knee.

"I don't know. It's like I got so used to being this enormous beast that I guess at some point I figured I'd always be this way. Like I'd be pregnant forever. But now that my water broke, it's like holy shit, we're going to have a baby! I don't know what to do with a baby," I squeaked out, starting to freak out. Jack laughed at my irrationality. "Don't laugh at me, damn it. It's not like you'll even be around."

That stopped Jack's laughter immediately. "That's not funny."

"I'm not trying to be funny."

"You want me to quit baseball? I'll fucking quit tomorrow," he offered, his tone serious.

I narrowed my eyes at him. "Of course I don't want you to quit baseball. But don't make fun of me when I'm freaking out, Jack. 'Cause I'm freaking out," I admitted. "I'm scared. I don't know what to do with babies."

"You'll be great, Kitten. You'll be amazing. And if you end up needing help, we'll hire a nanny. Hell, I'll hire you one for every day of the week if it helps. Whatever makes you happy."

"I do not want someone else raising our child! Are you crazy?" I started to yell. "It's not like I'm working anymore, so there's no reason I should need a freaking nanny to help me be a mom."

"Fine. No nanny." He glanced at me and then focused on the road. "It's funny how things work out, though."

"What are you talking about?"

"I was so unhappy about the trade at first, you know? But look at how it all worked out. You ended up being pregnant and we got to move home. Most of the guys aren't that lucky."

"Most of the guys don't want to be that lucky. They like

having their wives and kids in other cities. That way they can cheat without getting caught," I snapped.

"Whoa. Pregnancy's changed you."

"Isn't that the truth." He glanced at me with a raised eyebrow, surprised that I was completely in agreement, and I laughed. "I feel like a crazy person. Get this thing out of me."

He squeezed my thigh. "You have Gran and your mom," he said, then paused and added, "And Melissa. And my brother. We have a whole team here ready to help."

"You're right," I said, starting to settle down. "You're absolutely right. I'm sure I'll be okay. I'm just freaking out 'cause I've never done this before."

"I sure hope not."

Another contraction ripped through me, causing me to gasp.

"Kitten?" Jack's voice pleaded for a response, but I was too busy counting and trying not to hold my breath. When it ended, I unclenched his hand and he shook it out; apparently I'd been crushing his fingers. "I really don't like when you get those."

He fidgeted behind the steering wheel, his left knuckles almost white from his grip on it. "How bad do they hurt?" he asked, and then quickly changed his mind. "No. Don't tell me. I can't fucking handle hearing how much pain you're in." He huffed as he shook his head, changing his mind. "No. Tell me. What kind of man doesn't want to know how much pain his wife is in? The kind who can't do anything about it!" He slammed his hand against the wheel, his seesawing emotions clearly torturing him.

"Jack, stop. They aren't that bad, okay? They're just like sharp cramps. It's mostly uncomfortable," I lied. The contractions were getting stronger and longer, but Jack was right. There wasn't anything he could do for my pain and I didn't want him flipping out about it. It hurt me to see him react so defensively when it came to me. I reserved the right to protect my man the same way he wanted to protect me. And this was how I could do that, by avoiding the truth.

Jack glanced over at me, his face full of love and concern before he looked at the road again. "I can't just sit here next to you while you're gasping in pain and do nothing. It goes against everything I feel for you. It's my job to keep you safe and protected. I know it's illogical for me to think I can stop your labor pains, but my heart fucking feels like it's going to explode when I hear the sounds you're making. You being in pain doesn't fucking work for me, Kitten. It rips me in two the second it starts. It goes against every fiber of my being to sit there and pretend like I don't want to save you. I'd rather break my own hand again than know you're hurting."

I smiled, comforted by the depth of this man's love for me. "I understand completely and I love you for it. It's sexy as hell the way you love me, Jack. But I promise, I'm okay."

He pulled our car into the hospital parking lot, grabbed my overnight bag, and helped me out. "I'll carry you in if you want me to," he offered.

"I'm fine, really," I huffed as I waddled slowly. "I can walk."

He wrapped a protective arm around me and guided me toward the emergency room doors. Once we were all checked in, Jack demanded a room as quickly as possible, telling anyone who would listen that I was hurting, about to give birth at any second, and I needed to lie down. The nurses tried to calm him while I mouthed an apology to any of them who looked my way. They didn't seem fazed in the least, as if this type of behavior were an everyday occurrence in their department.

"Hi, Mrs. Carter. My name is Jane and I'll be your nurse for today. If you'll follow me, we'll get you all set up." The nurse's hair was meticulously pulled into a tight bun, not a hair out of place, and I found myself mesmerized by this fact. Jack was right. Pregnancy had made me weird.

"Please call me Cassie," I said, waddling behind her tiny frame down the long white corridor.

She paused in front of a wooden door and waved an arm. "We'll be in here."

"No one else is in here, right? She has her own room? I asked for a private room." Jack fired off the questions without taking a breath.

"Yes, Mr. Carter. She will have her own delivery and postnatal room per your request."

Jack walked into the room first and looked around, checking it carefully before heading back toward me.

"Sorry, he's a little, um—" I paused, searching for the right word.

"Nervous?" She smiled. "Most of the first-time dads are," she said, her voice gentle and comforting as she ushered us into the oversized hospital room.

Jack's strong arm guided me forward once again. "It's huge in here," I said, glancing around at the spacious room. The hospital bed was small in size, but the rest of the room was elegantly decorated much like a hotel would be, with bedside tables and a desk.

A light green couch with a hideaway bed sat under the only window. An oversized brown leather chair sat in one corner of the room, and all I could think about was how cold it looked. I'd never been a big fan of leather. It always creaked and moaned whenever anyone first sat in it.

Across the room in the other corner rested the most comfortable-looking rocking chair I'd ever seen. It complemented the decor of the room with its neutral tones, entirely covered in thick cushioning. I wanted to sit in that.

"We need to get you changed and hooked up to the monitors," Jane said as she pulled back the curtain suspended from the ceiling that surrounded the bed. "The bathroom's right through that door behind you. Your gown is folded up on the counter. Remember, the opening goes in the back." Jane smiled and pointed to the doorway before walking toward one of the machines.

I entered my private bathroom and changed as quickly as I could. Folding up my pajamas, I brought them out and handed them to Jack. He tossed them onto the couch into a messy pile, and I rolled my eyes.

Men.

"Do you need help into the bed?" Jack offered and I waved him off, climbing into it on my own.

Once I was lying down, I noticed the walls were painted a seafoam green color and it soothed me to look at them. Above my head was a stuffed mock headboard nailed to the wall, flanked by art glass pendant lights on each side. For a hospital room, this was pretty nice.

"Okay," Jane said efficiently. "I need to get the IV started first." She poked a large needle into my hand and I winced as soon as the fluids hit my bloodstream.

Looking up at her, I asked, "Is it normal for that to hurt?"

Jack tensed and looked hard at Jane, who said quickly, "Some patients report a burning sensation at first. But it should fade in no time."

I nodded with surprise. "You're right. It's already gone."

"Great. Now I need to wrap this band around your stomach. It's a bit uncomfortable because it's tight. It measures your baby's heart rate so we can monitor it during labor, as well as your contractions' length and strength."

"Okay." It pinched as she tightened it around the top of my belly.

"Is that all right?" she asked, cocking her head to one side.

"It's fine."

"Good. See the monitor here?" She pointed at the green machine with several small LCD screens to my right. "You can see when your contractions hit right here. And your baby's heart rate right here."

"Cool."

"Do you know what you're having?" she asked, looking between Jack and me.

"We do." I smiled at her before turning my head toward Jack, my eyes beginning to tear up. I didn't subscribe to the whole "we don't want to know the gender of our baby" way of thinking. My mind was far too organized for that sort of nonsense and I needed to be prepared for this little person entering our lives. Especially with the chaos that was Jack's baseball schedule, the idea of any more surprises did not sound appealing.

Jane continued to hook me up to various things, another monitor on my arm for my heart rate, as well as the prepping for an epidural if I wanted. Just a few days ago, I'd felt like a beached whale. Now I felt like a science experiment with wires coming out of me from all sides. I couldn't even walk to the bathroom without having to wheel the IV support with me.

I looked at Jack, who had moved the leather chair right next to my bed, and smacked my forehead with my hand. "Shit. I forgot to text everybody with the room number. Can you send them a text and tell them please?"

"Of course." He reached for my phone and stood up. Leaning down to give me a kiss, he whispered, "I love you," before kissing my belly and telling our baby the same. Then he walked around the curtain and out of my view, and I heard the door open and then pull to a close.

Two seconds later he was back in the room, a huge dimpled smile lighting up his face. "They're already out there."

"Who is?" I asked, completely confused.

"All the knuckleheads. They want to come in. Can they?" Jack directed his question toward our nurse, Jane.

She nodded. "They can come in until it's time to deliver. Or," she pointed at me, "until you want them out."

"Warn them that I look like ass!" I shouted toward Jack's back.

"You look beautiful, Kitten."

Our families wasted no time filling up the room, all nervously beaming at me in expectation. My heart filled with love as I looked at them all and said, "I can't believe you're all here. What if it takes me a hundred hours to have this kid?"

My mom walked over to me first, looking incredibly happy as she leaned down and squeezed me. "I wouldn't miss it for the world. I'm so excited," she admitted, and I wanted to cry.

"Where's Dad?" I asked, only half-surprised that he wasn't here.

"He's traveling for work," Mom said without meeting my eyes. "He said he'll try to get here as soon as he can."

I wondered briefly if she believed the lies my dad told. I knew he most likely wouldn't show up at the hospital, so I assumed she had to know this as well. Maybe she chose to live in denial? I couldn't care anymore. I had my own family to worry about and take care of.

My eyes locked on to Melissa's blue ones, then my gaze traveled down the length of her tiny frame to where her hand intertwined with Dean's. She made a face at me and I laughed. "Get over here," I insisted and she dropped Dean's hand and ran over.

"I can't believe you're having a baby," she said into my hair as she hugged me awkwardly.

"I know! I can't believe it took you ten years to hook up with Dean. You guys look really happy."

She pulled back and made a face at me. "How could you let me be such an idiot for so long?"

"Uh, you're sorta stubborn. And you don't listen." I puckered my lips at her.

"I know. But to think I could've been this happy that whole time? I just want to kick myself."

"So, you are happy?" I asked, reaching for her hand.

"The happiest. I never knew," she said, then paused to gain her composure. "I just never knew it could be like this." Her eyes began to glisten, then a few tears spilled over.

"I'm so happy for you. Don't screw it up," I whispered, my voice playful.

"My turn." Dean's voice cut through our whispers. He bumped Melissa out of the way with his hip and leaned down to hug me.

Everyone wanted to hug me but I could barely move, so it turned out to be this awkward grab thing that happened instead of a real hug. "Hurry up and make me an uncle, would ya?"

"Talk to the kid in the belly," I told him sarcastically. "Clearly, I'm ready." I opened my arms to point to all the machines and monitors attached to my body.

Dean leaned down to speak directly to my protruding stomach. "Come out, kid. We're all ready to meet you."

Jack faked a cough and Dean stood up straight. "Uh-oh, I think I'm pissing off the big guy. How shocking."

"Step away from the belly that doesn't belong to you, little brother," Jack said in a booming voice.

"Are you serious?" I called out with attitude, and Jack instantly appeared at my side.

"Very. Don't put your lips on my girl's stomach again unless you want to lose them," Jack said, and if I knew him, he was only half teasing.

"You have issues. You know this, right?" Dean joked back.

Gran and Gramps joined the Carter family party at my bedside and I finally did cry. "Thank you for coming. You didn't have to get up in the middle of the night to sit around for who knows how long."

"We know we didn't have to, dear," Gran said. "But we wanted to."

"Yeah," Gramps added. "It's not like we have anything else going on. It's boring at the house without you kids there."

I felt bad that everyone I loved was up at this ungodly hour. They couldn't do anything but wait, but they all assured me there was nowhere else they'd rather be. Honestly, I felt loved and special. It was a wonderful feeling.

Jane came into the room, glanced at my monitor, then shooed everyone back into the waiting room. And wait they did.

Jack and I sat alone, hand in hand, as we waited for the doctor to arrive. We watched the monitor, which gave us a heads-up that a contraction was beginning before I could even feel it, then he coached me through the breathing to help me relax so the contractions wouldn't be quite so painful.

Eventually the doctor swept into the room, making a grand entrance with a pudgy nurse in tow, and once he took over, the real fun began. After two hours of pushing and panting and a lot of cursing Jack's existence, our baby was finally born.

"It's a boy!" the pudgy nurse announced. "Would you like to cut the umbilical cord?" she asked Jack.

"Of course." He stood and took the scissors from the nurse, then cautiously snipped where she instructed him to.

I wanted to act surprised by her words, but I knew he was a boy and had the pictures to prove it. I remembered laughing during one of the ultrasounds our doctor had ordered, when the technician took her stylus and drew an arrow to what was obviously the baby's penis on the screen, then wrote, I'M A BOY! YAY!!!!!!! When she handed me the photo of the screen capture, I stuck it in my purse and hid it away from our family and friends so they wouldn't know the sex of the baby. Later that night when I'd called Jack to tell him, I kept waiting for an "I told you so" since he'd been insisting the baby was a boy all along. But he was smart enough to keep that thought to himself.

Jane took over from there, closing the freshly cut cord with a clip. "This will turn black and fall off on its own. Don't freak out when it does." She placed our wailing bundle of joy onto a tiny scale before swaddling him tightly and putting him into my arms.

She then grabbed a pen and started to write on a blue-trimmed bassinet card as she said out loud, "April tenth. Happy birthday to—" She paused and glanced my way, waiting for me to reveal the baby's name.

"Chance. Chance Thomas Carter."

"Ooh, I like that," she cooed. "We haven't had any Chances yet."

Turning my head to the left, I noticed that Jack's eyes were misty. He tried hard to fight off the tears, his gaze pinging between his newborn son's face and my own.

"I love you. I love you so much. You're amazing. And he's incredible," Jack said as he planted soft kisses against my forehead and gently touched the baby's tiny hand.

"He's perfect. Aren't you, Chance?" I tipped his eight-pound-three-ounce body toward my face and I breathed in his sweet baby scent.

"Chance Fucking Carter," Jack breathed out. "It has a nice ring to it."

I smacked Jack's shoulder with my free hand as I stared at Chance's perfect little face. The baby yawned widely, then opened his big blue eyes with incredibly long lashes and grabbed hold of my finger, grasping it firmly in his little hand.

Holding our baby in my arms for the first time was the most amazing feeling; the enormity of it almost took my breath away. We were parents. Jack Carter and I were officially someone's mom and dad.

"We did this. We made this," Jack said softly as he stared with pride at his son, no longer concerned with the drops that fell from his eyes.

"We did. He's perfect. I love you." I smiled, my heart filled with so much love I felt like it could burst at any moment and paint the room with it.

"Are his eyes going to stay blue?" Jack asked as he stared at the baby, and I giggled.

"Probably not. They could turn brown like yours, or green like mine. We'll know in a few months," I reminded him. "Most babies' eyes are blue when they're born."

I knew I'd felt lucky before, but in this moment, I'd never felt luckier. It was one thing to be blessed enough to actually find the love of your life, when so many people never do. It was something completely different to go through the fiery pits of personal hell with that person, then come through it on the other side and still get to marry them. Nevertheless, it was a blessing on a completely different level to create a whole other person with them. There was no doubt in my mind that nothing in our lives could ever be more beautiful than this moment.

Before today, I thought I loved Jack with all my heart, but having a child with him changed things. The kind of love I felt for Jack now was more than it ever could have been before today. It was as though my heart instantly multiplied in size and filled itself with more love for the very person I didn't think I could possibly love any more. Jack and Chance equally held my heart in the palm of their hands.

I looked at Jack and tears were rolling down his face. Expecting them to be tears of joy, I was surprised to see that he looked somewhat sad. I reached to touch his cheek, wanting to fix whatever was bothering him in this perfect moment. "Jack, what's wrong?"

He wiped at his face before staring at me, his chest rising and falling. "I love you so much."

"I love you too," I responded as he put a hand up to stop me.

"The moment I looked at our son," he said with anguish, "something inside me snapped. Like a light switch turned on or something and filled my heart up completely. It's a kind of love I don't know how to describe. See, Kitten, I love you with everything *that* I am, but it's like I love him with *who* I am. Does that make any sense?" He started to fidget and gripped at his hair.

Smiling, I nodded. "I get it completely, because I feel exactly the same way. I love you both so much, but it's not the same kind of love. The difference is that I *choose* to love you, but loving our son isn't a choice. It simply … is."

"Exactly. That's exactly it," he breathed out, but continued to fidget. Something was hurting him and it killed me to see him in any kind of pain. We were supposed to be celebrating, consumed by happiness, but something was wrong.

"Jack?"

He closed his eyes and shook his head, as if fighting off personal demons. When his eyes opened, another tear fell. This time he didn't move to wipe it off. I watched as it traveled the length of his cheek and passed his jawline before falling from his face completely.

Finally, he said, "I just don't get it. I don't understand. I mean, one look at our son was all it took for me to feel completely consumed by love for him. The need to protect him, fight for him, kill for him, it filled me up the moment he took his first breath."

I watched as he talked, not sure the direction his thoughts were taking him. Before I could form a coherent thought, he went on.

"But not once have I thought about leaving him. Or walking away. And I just don't understand how not one of my parents, but both of them, could see me and my brother, have these feelings for us, and then leave us alone. I'd rather die than leave him. Or you. Ever."

My heart broke in that moment for my man. Always so strong and determined, it was times like this when Jack's hidden vulnerability shone through and we both realized how battered his soul truly was. "Babe, I don't know what to say. Maybe they left because they loved you guys too much?"

He shook his head violently. "No! My dad left and never came back. He didn't even say good-bye; he just left. And my mother specifically told me it was because we were bad. She made sure I knew damn well why she was choosing to leave. The two of us were so bad, she couldn't take it anymore. That's not love."

"Maybe she was the bad one?" I ventured. "Maybe she thought once you boys got old enough, you'd see that she wasn't worth loving? I don't know, Jack. I don't know why people do the fucked-up things they do. But I will tell you this—your parents leaving might have been the best thing in the world for you and Dean."

He huffed out a disgusted sound and I continued. "Just hear me out. When they left, you got to be raised by two of the best people I've ever met in my life. And I know right now, in this beautiful moment, you can't ever imagine feeling anything other than absolute love for our son, but there will probably come the time when you'll want to kill him."

Jack shot me a glare and I laughed. "Not literally, but I'm sure he'll be a pain in the ass at some point and it probably won't be very much fun."

"But I'd still never want to leave," he insisted. "No matter how bad he is, I'd never give up like that. I'd never fucking walk away. Not from either of you." His head lowered as he stared at the floor.

"Baby, I know that. And that's why you're going to be such a good dad. He's lucky to have you as his father."

"I don't understand how anyone can just leave. How do you

walk away from this feeling and not have guilt consume you piece by piece?" He laid his head on my stomach, his tears wetting the thin sheet between us.

"I don't either." I reached for him, twisting my fingers through his dark hair, and tried to comfort him.

"I'll never do that to you. To either of you. I promise," he said fiercely, his breath hot on my stomach.

Stroking his hair, I said, "I know that. I believe you. I wouldn't have married you if I thought you would ever leave."

He turned his head to glance up at me. "You have a lot of faith, Kitten."

"No. I know my man. And I love and trust him. He's nothing like his parents. He's not built to leave."

"I like that. Not built to leave. Except when I left you before. I left you before." His hands covered his face as his past ate away at his happiness.

I wanted to stop him from reliving all of the nightmares. Especially about Chrystle and the things we'd already gone through. In my opinion, those things were dead and buried and held no meaning anymore.

"Jack," I said sternly, "that was a different time and place. You were doing the right thing. Even then, you were trying to do the right thing. None of that matters now."

"I promise I'll never leave you again. I promise."

"I know. Okay? I know." I patted his head, longing to bring him peace.

"Except for work," he said, his words muffled against my stomach. "Shit. I'll be gone all the fucking time for baseball."

I sucked in a long breath. "I know that too. I knew that

when I chose to marry you as well. Stop worrying about all these things, Jack. We'll make it through."

Jack lifted his head, pinning me with a resolute gaze. "I don't ever want to let either of you down."

"You won't. Stop being so hard on yourself. Look at our baby. He's amazing. He's going to worship you and look up to you and want to be a baseball player just like his daddy."

"I can't believe I'm someone's dad," he breathed out, his eyes wide.

"I can." I smiled at Jack with love and longing, wanting nothing more than to be in our new home with our baby. It felt like our lives together, as a family, were just beginning.

And I couldn't wait to get started.

Five Years Later

Hard to Have a Family on the Road

Cassie

Being a mom was hands down the best thing I've done in my life so far. I loved being home with Chance, but it was hard trying to travel with Jack's team the way I used to when it was just me. It wasn't easy to pick up and leave for a weekend when you had a baby or a toddler to pack for. So Chance and I pretty much stopped traveling with Jack on his road trips altogether. It was too much for me to have to book our separate travel, rent a car, find the hotel, and then figure out how to get to the ball field, all with a screaming kid in my arms.

Jack and I began to argue more, until I realized that it was all the traveling that stressed me and made me lash out. Once I stopped trying to be everywhere at once, I felt myself calm down. I realized that I couldn't be everything to everybody all the time.

Jack, on the other hand, started to flip out more. He hated that we weren't on the road with him, but he claimed to understand. I knew, though, that it bothered him more than he let on, he just didn't want me to feel guilty. It wasn't that Chance and I weren't at the games with him that bothered Jack, but the fact that our not going meant that Jack wasn't around Chance as much as he wanted.

Being an absentee father was Jack's worst nightmare. He really struggled with being gone so much, and said on more than one occasion that he felt like he abandoned me during the season. I reminded him that it wasn't true, but it still ate at him.

In the meantime, Chance and I tried to make every home game. Thankfully the team provided a day care for the players' kids during the games, which made attending Jack's games a lot easier for a few of those years. I could watch him pitch and not be concerned that Chance was bored or hot or not having a good time. He usually didn't want to leave when the game was over, not until he saw his dad's face waiting for him at the door. Then our little boy's eyes, which had turned chocolate-brown just like his father's, would light up as he sprinted toward his dad's open arms.

It was in those moments that I felt my heart melt into a ball of goo. I didn't think I'd ever get tired of watching Jack interact with our son.

Dean and Melissa got married a few years ago. He proposed to her exactly one year after that night I took her to Gran's and they finally worked it all out. I secretly worried that Melissa might have doubts and think it was too soon, but she had been smitten with Dean since the second she let him into her heart. Once she had fully committed to him, there was no going back for her. She knew he was the one.

They got married in December the next year with a lavish ceremony at the Four Seasons. Between her career and Dean's, it was a celebrity-filled affair, with guests ranging from professional athletes to A-list movie stars. It could not have been more opposite from my wedding with Jack, which is why it took so long to plan. Of course, they planned the ceremony during the off-season so Jack could be in the wedding. In fact, all three of us were in it.

Chance was the cutest ring bearer I'd ever seen, not to mention a little naughty, but he was a little young for the job. At almost two years old, he toddled over to Gran instead of walking down the aisle. He plopped the pillow onto Gramps' lap before hopping straight into Gran's arms and burying his face. When she tried to point at me or Jack and tell him to bring us the pillow, he refused and wrapped his tiny arms around her instead. Gramps met me at the front of the church and handed me the rings.

I knew my face had turned beet red by that point as I glared at Jack and mouthed, "He's your son."

Jack mouthed back, "I know," as I handed the minister the rings.

Melissa got pregnant almost immediately following their honeymoon, and when they had a little boy they named Coby, another Carter boy had joined the world. I feared for the girls who would have the pleasure of knowing them in the future. Since Chance and Coby were only two and a half years apart, the chances of them going to school together were high. I braced myself for those teenage years and tried not to think about it too hard or I'd never sleep again.

I thought I would miss working a lot more than I have. We've been so blessed to be in the position where I not only don't have to work, but I could most likely pick right back up from where I left off when I did decide to restart my business.

Not that I'd be working in New York, of course, but since I was a professional photographer with one hell of a portfolio, I could freelance when I was ready. But that wouldn't be for quite a while. Nora offered me a one-month gig in France recently, but I turned it down. She said she knew I would, but she wanted to offer it to me anyway.

Jack encouraged my going to France for the shoot since it was during his off-season, but I refused to leave my boys during those rare months we actually got to be a family unit. Being away from Chance and Jack for that long by choice wasn't something I was comfortable with. And since I didn't want to take any work during Jack's baseball season, I spent my time taking silly pictures of Chance and the ocean outside my office window. Maybe once Chance got older, I might consider traveling for shoots, but maybe not. Only time would tell.

I still woke up every morning feeling blessed for the opportunity to live in this house. There'd been more than one occasion where I'd walked the beach for hours, allowing my thoughts to get lost in the sand between my feet.

Chance fell in love with the ocean as soon as he could walk. He would spend all day playing in the sand if I'd let him, and I've stopped him from running straight into the water more often than not. No one told me how difficult it was to reason with a child. They simply don't have the understanding of fear the way we do.

In some ways I envied Chance's state of mind. I knew he was a child, but he was fearless and did things that adults would never do simply because he wanted to. The mom in me attempted to balance instituting some fear in him to keep him safe, while also encouraging his desire to try new things and be brave. Being a mom meant that each day I was challenged in a new way. It was the toughest, yet most rewarding job I'd ever have.

Jack was still playing for the Angels, although there was one year when talks of a trade scared us half to death. The thought of Jack moving to another state for eight months out of the year didn't sit well with either of us.

Thankfully they were just rumors that were reported nonstop on ESPN and the news, but weren't based on any facts. It was funny how often that kind of thing happened. So many things got leaked and talked about on the sports channels that had no factual basis at all. Not surprisingly, the mention of "a reliable source" was all those shows needed to give them the leeway to report whatever they wanted.

One day Jack's coach pulled him into his office, and Jack told me later that he'd braced for the news, terrified to have to tell me he'd be leaving again. But the coach only called him in to tell him that the rumors were false and they had no intention of letting Jack go.

"I was so scared when Coach called me in, Kitten. You have no idea," Jack confessed as we lay in bed that night.

"Oh, I can imagine," I breathed against his chest. "I'm so glad it was only rumors."

"They shouldn't be able to say shit like that."

"Daddy, bad word." Chance's tiny voice surprised us, coming from the doorway of our bedroom.

Jack and I immediately sat up. "You're right," Jack told him. "That was a bad word. What are you doing up, bud?"

"I had a bad dream," he confessed, dragging his tattered blue blanket behind him as he walked toward Jack's side of the bed. "Can I sleep with youse guys?"

I smiled and scooted away from my husband to make some space between us. "You bet. Get in here." Jack reached for him and helped pull him up onto our bed.

"Thanks, Mommy. Thanks, Daddy." He scrambled under the blankets and in no time fell back to sleep.

Jack stared lovingly at our little boy and said quietly, "I'm away from you two enough already. If they traded me I would have quit."

"What? No, you wouldn't have," I insisted. Not because I didn't want Jack to be home more, but because I didn't really believe him.

"This is my tenth season, Kitten. Full pension after I complete it. I've been thinking about it anyway."

"Thinking about what? Quitting?"

I couldn't imagine Jack not playing baseball. All I'd ever known was him being a ball player three hundred sixty-five days a year. It wasn't something he could turn off when he wasn't playing. He was always prepped, prepared, and working toward new goals.

All his hard work paid off. The amazing thing was, Jack actually did come back as strong as he once was. He was right when he'd insisted that he just needed time to fully heal. These days he consistently threw between ninety-three and ninety-four mile-per-hour pitches, just like before.

"I think this might be my last season."

I sucked in a shocked breath. Hearing those words from him both excited and terrified me. I didn't want Jack to go back to being who he was when he got hurt. That fear remained, even as I responded, "It's up to you. I'll support whatever you decide to do. Just be sure, okay?" I smiled reassuringly and rubbed his arm before turning out the light and snuggling next to our bed-hogging son.

But my eyes stayed open as my mind whirled, and it was nearly dawn before I fell into a fitful sleep.

You Miss Out

Jack

It had been five years since Cassie and I extended our family, since the birth of our amazing son, Chance. I loved Cassie more today than I did yesterday. And there was no doubt that I'd love her more tomorrow than I did right now. There seemed to be no end to my love for this girl.

She made me a better person. She was the mother of my child. There was no way I could explain how this made me feel about her. I only knew that my heart felt like it expanded daily to fit in all the love I had for her.

Cassie started missing the majority of my games; even the home ones as Chance got older. She did her best to attend every game I was scheduled to pitch for, whether she brought Chance or not. And she only traveled with me if Melissa and Dean watched Chance, but now that he was starting school, she felt extra guilty about leaving him at all.

I tried to convince her to bring him to more away games, but it was just too hard for her during the school year. And even when we played at home, it was usually on a weekday and that didn't fly with her. She insisted on giving Chance as much structure as possible, with a schedule that didn't include growing up at a ballpark.

Weekends were a different story, though. Thank God for weekend games. Although now that Chance had started playing Pony baseball, I wasn't sure how many of my games they'd be able to make.

I definitely played second string to my son. And you know what? I didn't mind at all. What I did fucking mind, though, was the fact that I missed out on all these things. My entire life had revolved around being at a baseball stadium, or traveling to one.

There was no need for anyone to tell me how good I'd had it, because I already knew. But no one ever told you how hard it really was to balance family with a baseball career. You know why they didn't tell you?

Because it was impossible.

There was no balance.

Baseball won every time.

Never getting days off to plan or celebrate anniversaries, holidays, or birthdays was one thing when it was just me and Kitten. It still fucking sucked and I felt like a dick, but Cassie never complained. Not once. But it was another thing entirely to miss out on your own kid's birthday. Every year since he'd been born, I'd missed his party. Sure, I got to relive each one in a series of photographs Cassie had taken. But it wasn't the same as actually being there.

Chance was getting ready to start kindergarten the next day. It was his first day of "big kid" school, as he liked to call it, and I was stuck in some swanky hotel in Arizona. I knew Cassie was fine without me, but I hated missing out on everything. Dialing her number, I couldn't help but smile when he answered the phone instead of her.

"Hello? Daddy?"

"Hey, bud. Getting ready for school tomorrow?"

"Uh huh. We're shopping right now."

"Oh, I see. Can you put Mommy on the phone?"

"No."

"Uh, why not?" I stopped myself from laughing.

"'Cause it's my turn to talk to you. She always gets to talk to you," he said matter-of-factly.

"You're right. But I need to tell her one thing and then she'll give you back the phone, okay?"

"Okay." His voice sounded deflated as he handed the phone to his mom.

"Hey, babe," she said with a giggle.

"What are you shopping for?"

"Oh my gosh, the school gave us a list of supplies he needs for his class. You should see the size of this thing. I'm walking around the store trying to find all this crap."

"Bad word!" Chance shouted in the background and Cassie apologized to him.

"Do you have any idea how weird it is to look at him and see you? He has your eyes, Jack. They make me miss you so much."

"I miss you too. I wish I were there. Take pictures of his first day and send them to me. Don't forget."

I'd insisted that Cassie do that with everything I missed. My phone's photo albums were filled with pictures of events and parties that I didn't get to see in real life, but got to experience via photo text message.

"I won't forget. Chance is pulling on my shirt. He wants to talk to you."

"I love you, Kitten. Miss you," I said before hearing the fumbling of the phone being passed over.

"Daddy, guess what?"

"What?"

He sucked in a big breath. "I start school tomorrow and Coby is mad because he can't come with me. He has to be in the baby school still and I get to go with the big kids."

I smiled. "So, you're excited?"

"Yep! 'Bye, Daddy. I love you," he said out of nowhere before hanging up on me. I sat on my hotel bed with my jaw slack.

The little shit.

My phone immediately beeped with a text.

Sorry. Guess he was done. LOL. I'll call you later. Love you.

Knowing that the list of shit he needed for school fell on Cassie's shoulders made me feel like a complete asshole. I started to feel like my heart was made of kite string, unraveling into a heap of nothing inside my guts. My dad walked out on me and my brother and never came back. My mom chose to leave us too. I would never leave my family, but how was I any better than my parents? I may not have left, but I was still never home.

I tossed and turned all night, trying to fall sleep. Instead of being focused on tomorrow's game, all I could think about was the fact that it was my five-year-old son's first day of school and I was going to miss it. The same way I missed everything else in our lives. Tugging at my hair, I had to force myself to stop from crying at the mere thought that I had a five-year-old already. Where had the time gone? How had five years flown by so fast?

I fucking hated being away from my family and I especially hated missing important days like this. It made me feel like a worthless absentee father with each event I continued to miss out on. Cassie never made me feel bad about it. No one did. Everyone claimed to understand, but I was the one who stopped being so forgiving.

The next morning my phone beeped, and I was greeted with a picture of Chance. He was looking at the phone with a crooked smile on his face, his dimple showing, his hair all spiked up, and an oversized backpack on his back. Or maybe the backpack was normal-sized and he just made it look big because he was so little.

Another beep and I clicked on my phone to open one more picture message. Cassie and Chance took a selfie together and my fucking heart squeezed inside my chest. I felt it contract and release as I stared at my beautiful wife and son. Her eyes looked so green and her smile was so big, I wanted to reach into the phone and pull her image right out of it. Chance's beaming face was pressed against hers as he gave me a thumbs-up.

Another big day missed. Another lost moment in time I'd never be able to get back.

Life was making me hate the one thing I'd always loved the most. Kitten excluded.

After our game that night, I called Cassie as we waited at the airport to catch our flight back. "How was it? Did he have a good day?"

She yawned. "He did. He made so many new friends and he told everyone that his daddy plays for the Angels. To be honest, I think his teacher has a crush on you. She was super googly-eyed when I picked him up today."

I laughed. "Sounds like a smart chick."

"I knew you'd say that. He has homework already."

"What? Since when did they start giving kindergartners homework?"

"I have no idea, but he has this ginormous packet that's due on Friday." A packet I'd never get to help with because I was never fucking home. "Jack?"

"I'm here."

"Are you okay? You sound upset."

"I'm good, Kitten. I'll see you soon."

"When will you be home?"

"Late. I won't wake you."

"No, it's okay. Wake me," she said in a soft voice. "I mean

it."

At her words, I instantly started to harden, so I glanced around to be sure no one was looking as I adjusted my pants. Half-tempted to hop into our plane's cockpit and fly myself back home, I paced the area of the private lounge instead. I didn't want to be here anymore, away from her. I needed to be home.

"What's up, Carter? You okay?" our starting catcher, Frank, asked me midstep.

I glanced at him sideways before blurting out, "I'm just tired of being gone all the time. Do you ever get like that?"

"Hell yeah, man. I hate being away from Christina and the kids. It's hands down the worst part about being a ball player." He downed the rest of his shot. "Well, aside from the politics and all the business bullshit that ruins this sport for us. Missing the little things like making lunches, helping with homework, science fair projects, and all their games completely sucks."

"Right? I feel like I'm coming apart at the seams. Like I can't live through another day missing all those firsts. Chance started kindergarten today and all I got was a picture. I missed his first day of school. It fucking kills me," I admitted.

"You need a drink." He waved the bartender over. "Scotch on the rocks."

"I don't drink scotch."

"You do tonight," he said flatly.

I shrugged, willing to try anything to help settle my soul.

"How many seasons is this for you, Carter?"

I knew what he was getting at. He wanted to know how close I was to the elusive tenth season. It was an unspoken thing we all reached for, that tenth season, which equaled full pension benefits. "Ten."

"What are you going to do when it's over?"

"I'm not sure," I lied. I knew exactly what I'd be doing when this season ended, but I wasn't telling my teammate before I informed my wife.

"It doesn't get easier. Just so you know," he said after finishing another drink. "It's always the same thing. Our wives are sitting at home raising our kids without their fathers. The absolute worst part is when Christina needs help disciplining the boys and I'm not there. They fight her and there's no one to help her keep them in line, you know? I feel like complete shit whenever she calls me crying."

That thought killed me and it wasn't even my family Frank was talking about. I wondered how he could be so calm about this. If Chance ever gave Kitten shit like that, I'd be on the first plane out to beat his ass. Or probably not. Because I'd get benched.

Fuck.

"Yet here we sit." I waved my arm around the darkened space. "In a private airport lounge waiting to fly home, instead of working a normal job like the rest of the world so we could be home with our families."

He smiled. "Eh. The rest of the world isn't lucky enough to get to do this for a living. And you know damn well that if they could do this, they would. No real man would walk away from this opportunity."

The hairs on my neck bristled as I formulated my response. "I don't think playing baseball makes you a real man. I think taking care of your family and being there for them is what being a real man is about."

He looked me directly in the eye. "But we are taking care of them, Carter. We're providing a life for them that most can't. I know we aren't home all the time, but there are plenty of men who travel for work for a living. And trust me, their jobs are nowhere near as cool as ours."

Frank was definitely a glass-half-full kind of guy and I was drowning in a glass-half-empty kind of night. "This isn't the life I wanted to provide," I said. My thoughts turned fuzzy as the scotch filled my head.

"Well, this is the hand you were dealt. A million other guys would gladly take your spot."

His comment pissed me off, but he was right. I couldn't have it both ways. I could either be a baseball player until I couldn't throw anymore, or I could be home with my family. Either way, I needed to stop bitching like a little girl. I sounded like Dean.

As soon as I got home, I turned off the light over the stove that Cassie had left on for me. I punched in my security code and dropped my bag to the floor before I crept up the stairs. Peeking in on my little stud, I leaned down to give him a peck on the cheek. His eyelids fluttered, but he didn't wake up.

Walking down the hallway into the master bedroom, I kissed my sleeping wife, then slipped my hand under her pajama top. She turned over and groaned. "Jack?"

"You expecting someone else?" I teased as her eyes opened.

"Maybe. What day of the week is it again?" She chuckled and I silenced her with my mouth. I nipped at her lips before she parted them so I could kiss her more deeply. Her tongue stroked against mine in a frantic dance. "I missed you."

"I missed you too. I'm sorry I'm always gone." I rolled on top of her and leaned on my elbows, so I could look down at her beautiful sleepy face.

"Don't apologize, Jack. I've told you a hundred times that I knew what I was getting into." Her hands cupped the sides of my face and I wanted to freeze this moment.

"But did you know I'd leave you alone when we had a kid? Did you sign up to be a single mom forever?"

"I'm not a single mom," she huffed out before nudging me to move over. "What do you want to hear, that it sucks sometimes? That I hate it when you aren't here? Because some days I do, Jack. I really do. Like when Chance does something so cute or says something super funny and I wish you were here to share that moment with me. And it's not just because you're missing the things that Chance does, but because I'm missing sharing them with you. I want to turn and look at you and laugh about how crazy our boy is, but when I look, you're not there. And those are the parts that make me sad."

If she wanted to break what little resolve I had left, she was doing a damn good job. "That's exactly what I'm talking about."

"But most of the time, I'm okay." She rolled onto her side to face me. "We're okay. And those moments when I get sad, they don't happen all the time. Of course I always wish you were here, but the really hard parts, they're just a flash. All right?"

"I didn't know I was marrying a superhero."

"You didn't? Who else would Harry Potter marry?" She laughed at the nickname she'd given me all those years ago. I couldn't believe it had stuck after all this time. I'm way hotter than Harry fucking Potter.

The End of a Dream

Jack

I'd never planned on keeping things from Kitten, but this was something I needed to do on my own. I mentioned to her at the beginning of the season about how I was thinking about this being my last one. She smiled and patted my arm as if to fucking placate me.

She definitely didn't think I was serious. But I was.

I am.

Lately I had begun to hate myself. I knew what I needed to do to save my family and my sanity; I had to make a choice. And there was really only one choice for me.

This whole season I'd been playing like it was the last time I'd be doing it. I said good-bye to every stadium and field as though I knew I wouldn't be playing on it ever again. I laughed more, enjoyed the game more, felt less stressed. It was so liberating to know in my heart that I was making this decision on my own terms.

I hadn't told anyone yet. Not my agents, not even Dean.

I'd reached that elusive tenth season and my pension was fully vested. It was a shit thing to make it about the money, but it wasn't really about the money, per se, it was about the security for my future. My family's future. I couldn't play this game forever, and as respected as I was, snot-nosed little rookies who threw faster than I ever did were being born every day. Who knew, maybe one day that would be my boy. Or my nephew.

I was finally ready to say good-bye to the one thing that had owned me almost my entire life. My mind flashed back to the day I got hurt and the weeks that followed. I'd come so far from where I was then. I remembered fighting within myself and the feeling of utter dread that my career might be over. But I didn't feel anything like that now. This decision, this moment, it felt right.

I fucking couldn't wait to tell my girl. And my boy.

What the hell was my family going to do when Daddy was home all year long? I'd probably drive them both crazy; Cassie would probably kill me in my fucking sleep. I was sure I'd deserve it, but I didn't care. I just wanted to be there.

Heading home after the game, my mind reeled with a sense of freedom. Admittedly, I dreaded letting my agents know I wouldn't be playing anymore, but this was my life and I needed to finally live it. I'd been an active participant in only parts of my life, but the other parts I'd been more like a distant cousin you only saw once or twice a year.

Throwing open the entry door from the garage, I was met with the sound of laughter coming from upstairs. "Where's my family?" I shouted toward the sounds.

"Daddy!" Chance screamed and hopped down the stairs two at a time. When he got to the bottom, he ran straight into my arms.

"Hey, buddy. How was your day?"

"Good! Mommy and I made chocolate chip cookies and I ate the dough."

"Hmmm," I said as my mouth watered. "Do you think Mommy saved any cookie dough for me?"

"Uh-huh." His head nodded rapidly up and down, and I placed my hand on top of it to slow it down. "She put some in a box for you," he added slyly.

"A box?" I gave him a funny look as Cassie walked into the kitchen.

"He means a container. It's in the fridge. Hey, babe." She pressed her mouth against mine and I almost forgot we had an audience until he tugged at my shirt.

"Daddy, will you swim with me? Mommy said I had to wait until you got home to swim. But now you're home. Let's swim. Please. I wanna swim."

My eyes widened as he talked a hundred miles a minute. "Sure thing. Just let me talk to Mommy for a second, okay?"

His shoulders slumped as he said dejectedly, "Okay."

Cassie kneeled down so that she was eye to eye with him. "Why don't you run upstairs and go put on your swim trunks and grab your floaties, okay?"

Chance's lip jutted out into a pout. He had Cassie's mouth. "I don't need my floaties, Mom!"

She stood up and put her hand on her hip. "Chance. If you don't get your floaties, you can't go in the pool. You know the rules."

"Never go in the pool without floaties or an adult," he

recited in a monotone voice, and I suppressed a smile as I realized I had a lot of rules to learn.

"That's right. Now, go get changed. Daddy will meet you in your room as soon as we're done talking."

"Okay!" His mood instantly improved, Chance took off running up the stairs, leaping with excitement from the left side of one stair tread to the right side of the next, just for the sheer joy of it.

"Holy shit, babe, he's exhausting," Cassie said. "He's like the Energizer bunny. He's never tired. Ever." She blew out a breath and wiped her forehead with the back of her hand.

I took her hand and pulled her close as I reconsidered what I was about to tell her for two full seconds before blurting it out. "I've officially decided that I'm not playing after this season." Holding her against me, I prayed she'd be excited as I waited for her response.

Cassie's eyes lit up, but she held back a smile as she asked cautiously, "Are you sure?"

I nodded. "I told you at the beginning of the year that I thought it would be my last. I went into this season thinking that and I've mentally said my good-byes to everything and everyone. I'm ready to leave," I said, and was happy to realize that I really meant it.

"Jack, if you're ready to leave, then I can't wait to have you home." She smiled as the tears welled in her eyes.

Sighing with contentment, I pulled her closer and buried my face in her hair, inhaling the fragrance of her shampoo. The feel of her body pressed against mine not only aroused me, but comforted me as well. This girl was my life. I was holding my life in my arms and as long as I had her, I knew I'd be okay without baseball.

"I can't wait to be home, Kitten," I said into her hair. "I've missed so much. I don't want to miss any more. And the nastiness of the business, it's just not worth it."

Cassie knew what I meant. The business side of the baseball industry had the potential of souring your entire experience if you allowed it to. I wanted to leave on my terms, before I not only hated myself, but the sport as well.

"You're sure? One hundred percent certain this is what you want?" She tilted her head back and looked me in the eyes.

"Without a doubt. And you know what the best part is?" I asked, and watched as her long blonde hair swayed as she shook her head. "I feel relieved."

"Then you know it's right." Her smile grew as she pushed her lips to mine and pulled me hard against her. When she broke the kiss she asked, "Does Dean know? Or Marc and Ryan? Do they know?"

"Not yet. They've been fielding offers from other teams lately since my contract's up. There's been some pretty great offers, but I haven't even considered them."

"Daddy, I'm ready!" Chance shouted from the top of the stairs.

"Be right up. Give me two seconds," I shouted back and watched as he kicked at the railing. "Don't kick the railing please, buddy." He stopped and dropped to his butt, his legs folded Indian-style as he waited for me.

"You should probably tell Dean in person," Cassie suggested. "Want me to invite them over for dinner? Coby loves swimming in the pool."

"Actually, that sounds great. Can we invite Gran and Gramps too?"

"Of course. I'll call everyone. You go swim with your boy."

Giving her a quick kiss, I bolted upstairs to change.

Cassie handled everything while I swam in our saltwater pool with Chance. He splashed and kicked, but mostly he wanted me to throw him around. Playing in the pool with this kid was almost a better workout than the gym. My shoulders ached by the time Dean and Melissa arrived and my little nephew jumped in the water, begging for me to throw him too.

"Frow me, Unckie Jack. Frow me!" Coby screamed out in excitement, his cheeks turning bright red.

I grabbed him and tossed him into the air as he squealed. His little face popped right back out of the water as soon as he entered it. "That vest thing you're wearing is pretty cool," I said to Coby, impressed with the floatation devices kids these days had to wear.

"That's for little kids. I'm wearing big kid floats," Chance informed me as he touched one of the inflatable bands he wore around his arms.

My brother, Dean, appeared out of nowhere and dove straight in, splashing everyone in the pool. He swam over to where the three of us were and gave me a nod.

"Are kids always this competitive?" I asked him after I

tossed our kids into the water again.

"I don't know about all kids, but ours sure are."

"We weren't like that," I insisted as I tried to remember being that way with Dean growing up.

He laughed. "No, what you mean to say is *I* wasn't like that. You were definitely like that."

"Was not."

"Was too."

"We'll ask Gran then."

"Ask me what?" Gran's voice caught our attention and I hopped out of the pool before drenching her in a wet hug. "Jack! Stop it."

"Gran's all wet!" Chance shouted. "Daddy, you got Gran all wet. I wanna get Gran all wet." He clambered out of the pool and ran into Gran's legs, soaking her pants.

"Chance, no running!" Cassie called out from the open window.

"Sorry, Mommy!" Chance yelled as he ran/walked back to the pool and jumped in.

Gran eyed me like she was going to kill me and I played innocent. "I can't help it that all the boys love you. You should really blame yourself."

"Nice try." She waved a finger at me. "Now, what were you boys talking about?"

"Gran, Jack seems to think that we weren't competitive growing up," Dean said in a mockingly shocked tone as Gran giggled.

"Obviously Jack has a selective memory. Honey, you were extremely competitive with Dean. But he wasn't competitive back. He just wanted to be like you."

"Told you." Dean splashed me before diving under the water.

"Uncle Dean, throw me!"

"Frow me too, Daddy!"

"Me first, Uncle Dean!"

I watched as Dean tossed our kids into the air one at a time before they splashed into the water below. Their excited squeals filled the air and I wondered if there were any greater sound than the sound of your family laughing together.

"You've built a beautiful life for yourself, Jack," Gran said softly. "I couldn't be more proud." My grandmother leaned against me and slipped her arm around my waist.

"Thanks, Gran. I wouldn't be half the man I am today without you and Gramps. Thank you for all you've done for me. And for Cassie. I don't know where'd we be right now if it wasn't for you two."

She wiped at her eye. "Oh, stop. You'd be exactly where you are right now. It just might have taken you both a little bit longer to get there."

"You think so?"

"Absolutely. You two were made for each other. You would have found your way there eventually. You're like magnets, each one pulling at the other until you connect, unable to pull apart."

"What about that knucklehead and his wife?" I pointed at Dean and she whistled.

"I'm not sure those two would have ever got their stuff together if Cassie didn't drag the tiny one over to our house that night. We'd probably still be waiting for them to work it out."

I had to agree. "So you're to blame," I teased and gave her a slight nudge.

Cassie and Melissa walked into the backyard side by side, whispering and laughing about who knows what. Gramps followed close behind, his eyes searching for Gran. He walked over and staked his claim.

"Get off my woman, young man."

"Now I know where I get it from," I said with a chuckle.

"Get what?" he said innocently.

"The desire to piss all over my property," I informed him with half a grin.

"I do not want to piss all over your grandmother, Jack," he started to say before Gran cut him off.

"A woman can only take so much. If either of you need me, I'll be with the outnumbered gender in the kitchen, where we belong." She sauntered over toward the girls.

"Kitten, did you hear that? Get your ass in the kitchen where you belong!" I hollered and she scowled at me.

"Bad word!" echoed from the two tiny mouths in the pool.

"I'm sorry," I shouted at them before jumping back in.

The ladies didn't disappear for long before they were all demanding we leave the pool and come get ready for dinner. They promised that we could swim after dinner, but we needed to eat first.

Our dining room table was set for eight and I couldn't remember the last time I'd felt this relaxed and genuinely happy. Cassie set down separate bowls filled with pasta and spaghetti in the center of the table, before asking everyone what they wanted to drink. Melissa added a basket filled with garlic bread to the mix, and Gran followed carrying a huge salad.

I loved these women. Even Fun-Size.

Cassie steered Chance toward one of the middle seats and pulled back the other middle seat across the table for Coby. Coby sat in some sort of booster chair thing, while Chance grabbed a stack of books from his room. I laughed as he carried them down, stacked them neatly on top of his chair, and then couldn't get up.

"Help me please," he asked in his raspy little voice.

I lifted him up and placed him firmly on the mountain of books. "He won't fall?" I asked no one in particular.

"He might," Cassie answered.

"I'm not gonna fall," Chance insisted as I scooted his chair closer to the table.

Gran and Gramps sat at the head of the table while my son sat between my wife and me. I was forced to stare at my brother's ugly mug throughout the whole meal.

"It was really nice of you to have us all here for dinner," Gran said in our direction. "Thank you for inviting us."

"Yeah. I love coming here for meals. Especially if Gran's cooking," Melissa added, taking a huge bite of bread.

Cassie leaned forward to give me an encouraging look, and I nodded.

"Well," I began, "we wanted you all here because I have some news. And I wanted to share it with everyone at the same time."

All eyes focused on me as the room went silent. Even the boys stopped fidgeting for a second. "I've officially decided that this will be my last season playing baseball."

Suddenly, several voices all rang out at once, each trying to talk over the other. Cassie raised her arms in the air to quiet them down. "Let him finish."

I looked around and scrunched my face before clarifying, "I was finished."

Dean's fork clanged against his plate. "But what about all the offers? You won't even consider them?" He suddenly turned from a brother to an agent.

"It's not about the offers," I said, then my tone turned firm. "I've made up my mind."

"But these are major league, starting rotation offers, Jack. Really solid contracts."

"I don't care, Dean."

Melissa reached over Coby and settled her hand on top of Dean's arm. It seemed to bring him back to reality and remind him who he was; my brother, not my agent.

"Why now?" Gramps asked, and I felt it was a fair question.

"Honestly? Because I think if I spend any more time playing, I'll lose it. I'll lose it all. The love I have for the game. The respect I have for the office that runs it. I'm tired of all the bullshit that goes on behind the scenes."

"Bad word, Daddy!" Chance yelled.

Coby giggled. "Bad word, Unckie Jack!"

"Sorry, guys." I really needed to watch my language around the boys. This was going to be an adjustment.

Shaking off my mental list of things to do once I retired from ball, I continued. "But I'm mostly tired of not being around. These past five years have been the hardest ones for me.

I might be a success on the baseball field, but I've felt like a failure at home."

"Jack." Cassie pushed her chair back and wrapped her arms around me from behind. She planted a kiss on the side of my head. "Nothing about you is a failure, do you hear me?"

I wanted to believe her, but I knew it sucked handling everything alone. Whether she wanted to admit it or not. "I appreciate you saying that, Kitten. I do. But it's hard not to feel like one."

"Well, knock it off." She smacked my shoulder before returning to her seat.

"Yeah, Jack," Gran said sternly. "Don't do that to yourself. You haven't done anything wrong. You've been a good husband and a good father while you also juggled a demanding career. No one faults you for that." The wonderful woman who raised me looked at me, her eyes filled with an odd combination of pride and sadness, and I felt a little twinge in my gut.

"You're a good person, Jack. I know you don't always believe that about yourself, but you are. I'm proud of you, son," Gramps added and I almost fucking lost it. If my brother and Melissa hadn't been sitting at the table, I probably would have cried like a baby, but I refused to do that in front of them. Dean didn't need to witness what a complete pussy I'd turned into.

"I want to be a better husband and a better father. And this is what I need to do it. I hope you all understand." I chanced another glance at my brother.

"Playing baseball on a professional level is intense, bro. You've given up so much to do it, you always have. If you think about it, you've never really had a normal life. You've always been busting your ass to make your dreams come true. And once they did, the work didn't stop, it only got harder." Dean nodded thoughtfully. "It's your career and I think it's pretty awesome if you end it on your terms."

"Thank you. Do you think Marc and Ryan will be pissed?"

"Nah." He waved me off. "Surprised, maybe, but not pissed. They'll understand."

"Congratulations, Jack," Melissa chimed in. "You have no idea what you've been missing."

"But I do. That's the whole point."

"No, you don't. Not really. Do you even know what summer is? Aside from prime-time ball-playing season?"

I laughed. "I have a vague recollection of this thing you call summer."

Cassie squeaked as she inhaled sharply. "Oh my gosh! You'll be here for the fourth of July. And we can have barbeques all summer long! And swim parties! Jack, do you know what this means?" Her eyes practically glowed as she stared at me.

"Yeah, Kitten. That's what I've been trying to tell you. I'll get to have a life with you. An actual non-baseball-driven life. Better get used to me being around, because I plan on stalking you for quite a while."

"Dad, what's stalking?"

I shot Cassie a freaked-out look. "Uh, it's when you follow Mommy around the house all day."

"Ooooh," Chance said with wide eyes. "I stalk Mommy all the time."

Everyone at the table laughed and I felt like the luckiest guy in the world, surrounded by family and the people I loved. I couldn't wait to start the next chapter of my life.

Our New Lives

Cassie

I kept asking Jack if he was sure and he continued to insist that he was. If he changed his mind, I wanted him to know it was okay. The truth was, I hadn't gotten my hopes up super high, just in case he decided at the last minute that he couldn't retire. I would have understood. It seemed almost harder for me to grasp the concept that Jack was truly okay with quitting baseball, than it was for me to be mad at him if he reversed his decision.

But after he sat me down and told me he had officially decided to quit, his entire demeanor changed. It seemed like some virtual weight neither of us even knew existed had been lifted from his shoulders. He smiled more and got excited at the simplest things, like going to the movies. He couldn't remember the last time we'd done that. And sadly, neither could I.

Even during those few months of the year when it was considered the off-season, Jack was never truly off. A real baseball player couldn't be. This sport demanded so much of one's time and mental energy. He was always focused and that put everything else on the back burner, especially having fun with no consequences or guilt. I'd never realized it really …

until now.

Jack played his last game at Angel Stadium to a screaming, sold-out crowd. My parents showed up for the first half of the game before my mom complained about a migraine coming on and needed to leave. My dad offered to stay, but I told him that someone needed to drive Mom home and I wasn't leaving. He nodded before taking her by the hand. It was nice to share this moment with them, however briefly, and I thanked them for coming.

Chance gave them both huge hugs and kisses on the cheek. He loved my parents and that honestly made me happy. No matter how they'd disappointed me in the past, I wanted my son to have a good relationship with them. They weren't bad people at heart and I knew that. My dad seemed to be making an effort, and had been a man of his word lately. I figured now was as good a time as any to start mending those parental fences.

When the game ended, every single person in the stands rose to their feet and gave Jack a standing ovation. They chanted "Carter" throughout the innings and I was in tears pretty much the entire night.

Chance didn't understand why I was crying, but he loved watching his dad pitch. His eyes were so focused and intense and I recognized that gleam. I was certain we had a future ball player on our hands. Although every time the crowd screamed for Jack, Chance covered his ears and exclaimed, "It's too loud!"

Knowing this was the last time I'd ever be in this stadium watching Jack play made me want to throw up. The life we'd always known up until now was ending and I had no idea what to expect.

I'd be lying if I said I wasn't nervous. It wasn't that hard to think back to the time when Jack broke his hand and how mean he'd become. There was a part of me that was terrified to even entertain the idea of him acting like that again. What if he completely changed after tonight? What if he hated being free from baseball and didn't know what to do with himself?

I worried.

But all I could do was hope he'd made his decision for the right reasons and that he never blamed or resented me or Chance for them.

Melissa reached over and grabbed my hand. "It will be fine."

"What will?"

"I know what you're thinking. You're worried. Your face always does this little crinkle thing right here," she pointed at the bridge of my nose, "when you're worried. It will be fine. Jack will be fine."

"What if he hates me and thinks I ruined his life?"

"Do you hate him and think he ruined your life?" she fired back.

I frowned at her hard. "No. Why would I think that?"

"Because you had to quit your job and move out here to be with him. You haven't worked in almost five years. Do you blame him for that?"

"Not at all."

"He won't either."

I closed my eyes and knew she was right. "Thanks, Melis."

"I don't know why you don't just talk to me in the first place. You'd save yourself a lot of brow-furrowing."

I chuckled. "Remind me next time."

"I shouldn't have to remind you. Hell, if you don't know how smart I am by now, you'll never learn."

"Probably true," I admitted with a smile.

"Let's go get that husband of yours," she said as she tugged me out of my seat and led the way to the tunnels.

The seven of us walked down into the corridor and waited for Jack to come out of the locker room. I worried that it might be a long night since it was his last. His teammates would want to tell him good-bye, and I knew that there were reporters waiting to interview him as well.

I stood in the corridor, holding my son's little hand. At five years old, he still let me hold his hand in public, and I loved that. I dreaded the day he'd pull his hand away from mine and tell me he wasn't a baby anymore.

"Think he'll be long?" Dean asked, carrying his two-and-a-half-year-old son in his arms.

I nodded. "Probably. It's the last time he'll be in there, so we might be waiting all night."

Chance tugged at Dean's shirt. "Uncle Dean. Uncle Dean."

Dean glanced down at his nephew. "Yeah, little guy?"

"Put Coby down. I wanna play with my cousin," he demanded and Dean leaned over to do exactly that.

"Be careful, he's wobbly," Dean warned.

"What does wobbly mean?" Chance asked with a frown.

Melissa leaned down so she was eye to eye with him. "It just means that sometimes when he runs, he'll fall down. So don't chase him too fast, okay?"

"Okay, Aunt Lissa."

Chance and Coby ran around in circles between the other players' wives and relatives. The other families gave us sad smiles, each probably convinced that Jack didn't get any offers worth taking and that was why he was leaving. I smiled back, a huge, happy smile, which seemed to puzzle them. They didn't get it. But they didn't need to. This wasn't about them. It wasn't about anyone other than Jack and our family.

When the door swung open, I found myself shocked to see Jack waltzing through it, carrying a large duffel bag.

"Daddy!" Chance pulled his hand from mine and ran toward Jack.

"Hey, you." He planted a big kiss on Chance's cheek. "Did you like the game? We won."

"No. It was too loud and it hurt my ears. And Mommy cried."

Jack's eyes were instantly on mine. "Why'd you cry?"

"I was moved, Jack. The way the crowd reacted to you. It was really emotional for me to watch."

He leaned in and kissed my cheek. "It was emotional for me to watch too."

"Did you cry?" I asked a little too loud and he looked around.

"No. Who do you think I am, Dean?"

"I heard that," Dean called out as he chased his son around.

Melissa snuck up behind Coby and grabbed him as he screamed.

"I got you!" She held on to the wiggly toddler as Dean bent down to kiss her. She reached for his hand and leaned into him, which made me smile. I loved seeing them so happy.

Gran and Gramps sidled up next to me, tears in their eyes. I nodded their way, saying, "See, I'm not the only one who was moved to tears tonight," doing my best to divert the attention away from me.

"We're just so proud of you, Jack," Gran said as she allowed the tears to fall. Jack pulled her in for a hug.

"Thank you for being here. It means a lot to me."

Gramps slapped Jack on the back. "We wouldn't miss it for the world, kid."

"Are you ready to go, babe?" I asked my husband and he nodded. "Jack's ready," I announced to our small group. "We'll see you all at the house."

"We'll bring Chance with us," Melissa offered and I enthusiastically agreed. Sometimes it made life easier to get a little break.

After another round of hugs, Jack and I walked hand in hand out of the underground tunnels for the last time. Passing by a lone reporter, Jack stopped to shake his hand, and dropped his duffel bag on the ground.

"Jack, do you have a comment? Something to leave your fans with?" the familiar reporter asked.

"Hey, Casey. You remember my wife, Cassie." Jack introduced me to the reporter, but I couldn't place him exactly.

"Nice to see you again, Mrs. Carter. I bet you're excited to have Jack home full-time now."

"You have no idea." I squeezed Jack's arm and smiled.

"So, how about that quote, Jack? Anything you want to say to memorialize your career?"

Jack grew silent and I knew he was deep in thought. He took a deep breath before saying, "It's one hell of a sledgehammer to the chest when your baseball career comes to an end. It's like you finally realize that baseball never loved you back. All the sleepless nights, the hours spent at the gym trying to stay fit, the conditioning, the training, the mental preparation, the holidays missed, the birthdays passed, the memories you didn't get to make with your family … all for what? It's not like baseball lost any sleep over you. She didn't stay awake for nights on end, trying to figure out how to make you a better player. She didn't care. Baseball's a business. A sport. A game. And as much as my entire life has been wrapped up in it, it's time to let it go."

"So, is it safe to say that you're quitting for your family?"

Jack squeezed my hand. "It's safe to say that I'm quitting for me. I want to know what it's like to have a life outside baseball while my body can still do the things I want it to, knock on wood. I want to experience a weekend that isn't filled with hitting, pitching, fielding, working out, or meetings."

He flashed me a big smile, and said, "I want to wake up in the morning and not worry about whether or not my hand is going to tighten up today or if I'm still playing well enough to stay on the team that I love. I've given so much time and energy to this sport, but now it's time for me to give the same attention to my wife and son. I'm ready to have a life that includes them all the time, not just three months out of the year."

My heart squeezed inside my chest as the blood started pumping wildly in my veins. Every single thing this man did filled me with pride and love.

"Thank you, Jack. And congratulations. You're a hell of a player."

"Thanks, Casey. That means a lot coming from you."

The two men shook hands before Jack led me away from the stadium. I fought the urge to cry as we pulled out of the parking lot for the last time.

"It's so weird to think of you without thinking about baseball."

He glanced at me. "You think it's weird for you, how do you think I feel? I have to figure out who I am all over again."

"You know who you are."

"A man in love with his Kitten?"

I gave him a mock frown. "Jack, be serious."

"Part of my identity for as long as I can remember is being a baseball player. If I'm not that anymore, then who am I?"

"Who do you want to be?"

"Harry Potter," he teased.

I laughed out loud and grabbed his hand. "Mission accomplished."

Two Months Later ...

I didn't know what to do with myself with all the free time Jack's help gave me. It made me realize that I had been living a sort of single mom life, although I'd never admit that to Jack now. It served no purpose. I simply made sure to thank him for everything he was doing to help.

Longing to make up for lost time, Jack refused to let me help with Chance's homework, and woke up every morning to drive him to school. He even called Nora behind my back and told her I was ready to start taking on assignments. I had to tell Jack to "slow his roll." Yes, I wanted to work again someday, but not the second after he had stopped.

"You're trying to get me out of the house," I said after learning that he reached out to Nora.

"I don't want you to waste any more time not working now that I'm home," he confessed. "I can handle everything here just like you did. You put your dreams on hold for me, and now it's time you go chase them again."

My hand flew to my open mouth and covered it. Jack never ceased to amaze me when it came to how thoughtful, caring, and loving he was. Lowering my hand, I said, "Staying home with my son isn't a waste of my time. And now that you're here too, I'm in no rush to be gone."

"Are you sure? You've given up so much," he started to

say.

I shook my head. "I've given up nothing. My dreams aren't gone. They'll still be waiting for me when I'm ready to pursue them again. But that's not now. Especially not now." I couldn't imagine focusing on a job now that Jack was finally home. I wanted to take the time to enjoy actually being a family in a two-parent household.

"Well, that's good to hear because I've been gathering all these quarters, you see, and I can't really use them if you're not here to use them on."

"Is that so," I asked as I pressed my body against his chest and felt the need between my thighs.

"I have. I think I'll spend this whole jar right now. Knock you up again."

"I swear to God, Jack. If you give me another boy, we might need to adopt something female. Like a girl dog or something. All the testosterone around here is killing me. Between you and Dean and the boys, there are way too many Carter males running around."

He laughed hard. He does that a lot lately, thank God.

Touching his cheek, I said, "I'll never get tired of hearing that laugh or seeing those dimples."

"Better get used to it, Kitten. 'Cause I'm not going anywhere."

"I'm counting on it."

He leaned down and pressed his lips against mine, then deepened the kiss in that way that always made me want to tear his clothes off. I always assumed that if Jack changed after quitting baseball, it would be for the worse. It never occurred to me that post-baseball Jack might actually be better. There was a whole other person who lived inside him that neither of us knew existed. This guy was much happier, much friendlier, and a hell of a lot less stressed.

Not that Jack wasn't any of those things before he left, but like I said before, a weight had been lifted from my man's shoulders. He finally felt like he could let loose and have fun, actually go out on the weekend and not be wracked with guilt over it.

Quitting baseball had been one of the best decisions Jack ever made. And leaving the sport didn't make him miss the game, it made him love his life and the choice he made to finally have one. I loved my husband with every fiber of my being, and slept in his arms each night knowing he felt the same for me.

He'd promised to have me knocked up again by the end of winter. "It's my new goal," he said with a laugh.

"Consider it met." I chewed on my bottom lip as he pulled back from my arms.

"W-what?" he stuttered. "Do you mean what I think you mean?"

I tilted my head to the side and smiled. "If you think I mean that we're pregnant again, then yes."

Jack wrapped his arms around my middle and lifted me off the ground, the world spinning beneath my feet. "Oh my God, Kitten! Yes! I love my swimmers!"

I laughed, pulling out of his grip and touching my toes to the floor. "Your swimmers? You love your swimmers?"

Shrugging, he added, "I love you too. But you know that.

I'll always love you. Always." He lowered himself to his knees and pressed his lips against my belly. "And I love you too, little man."

Rolling my eyes, I whined. "Not this again."

Jack rose to his feet. "Yes, this again." He placed a gentle kiss on my lips. "You've seen us Carter men in action. We breed boys."

"You're gonna be in a lot of trouble, mister, when you find out we're having a girl."

"Never going to happen," he responded overconfidently, and I smiled.

Heaven help me.

Epilogue

Chance

Eleven Years Later …

All my life, I'd heard Uncle Dean's stories about what a stud my father was in high school, and how the girls all fawned over him. To be honest, not much was different with me. People always patted my back like I was a fucking champion or something as I walked through the school campus, and this afternoon—a game day—was no different.

Once I reached the locker room, I changed into my baseball gear, ignoring the rest of my teammates while I prepped mentally. Every game day, I followed the same routine: I changed into my gear in silence, refusing to say a word, while I listened to the "warm-up" soundtrack I downloaded blasting in my ears.

Heading out toward the baseball field, I spotted my dad in the bullpen, working with our starting pitcher. Since my dad started coaching the varsity baseball team at my high school, it became the school to attend … especially if you were a pitcher. Which I wasn't.

My dad had coached all my baseball teams except one since quitting the major leagues. To be honest, I only had vague memories of my dad playing baseball for the Angels. My childhood memories consisted mostly of my dad always being around, not him being on the road playing ball.

I decided when I was just a little tyke that I wanted to be a catcher. Maybe it was all the years of catching for my dad while he pitched balls at me? I didn't know for sure, but what I did know I was a great catcher. I had an arm like a cannon. Base runners didn't steal on me, I'd throw them out quicker than shit. Like a rocket launcher was attached to my arm, I'd fire that ball from behind home plate to second base and get them out nine times out of ten. My parents worried about my knees, but I worked hard to keep them strong and flexible. I knew all about what my dad went through when he got hurt in the majors.

Before I stepped into the dugout, I made a visual sweep of the stands and saw my mother was sitting alone on a stadium chair among the growing crowd. Since my cousin Coby was the only freshman who made the junior varsity team and our games overlapped, Uncle Dean and Aunt Melissa missed almost all of mine. Poor Gran and Gramps were forced to split their time between games, meandering back and forth between the two ball fields.

I scanned the crowd for my little sister, Jacey, only to see her talking to some boy who looked a year or two older than her.

Hope to God Dad doesn't see that.

Dad already had enough heart attacks with Jacey to last a lifetime, starting with her trying to wear makeup like she was twenty instead of ten, and coming down the stairs to go out wearing short shorts and little tank tops. Every time it happened, Dad would stand there with his face all red and his hand over his heart as he ordered her to march right back upstairs to change, while my mom just stood there and laughed.

My parents always got along really well. Every fight I'd ever seen them have always ended with a kiss and my father calling my mother by her pet name, Kitten. I'd find it kind of cute if it didn't make me want to fucking barf watching my parents make out like teenagers. There were some things you could never un-see.

No one knew why my dad called her Kitten, even though I'd asked about a million times. I couldn't even look at a kitten without thinking about my mom, which was pretty fucked up, if you asked me. And don't get me started on the deal with the quarters, either. I blocked out the real reason they collected them and chose to think about the stupid cutesy stories instead. Do you have any idea how weird it was to grow up thinking that quarters were meant to be put into jars and not spent? I almost had a coronary the first time one of my friends pulled a quarter out of his pocket and deposited it into a vending machine. As a matter of fact, I got a little hysterical, and the principal was forced to call my mom because I refused to calm down. She had to come get me and take me home. To this day, I ask for my change in dimes and nickels. No quarters for me.

No girls either. Unlike my dad, who was apparently some grade-A womanizing badass, I tried to steer clear of girls. They were distracting, and a pain in the ass. I had no idea how my dad got them to leave him alone, but if I so much as kissed a chick, I couldn't shake her for months. Didn't fucking need that.

"Chance! Get out here and warm up that arm, son!"

I headed out of the dugout and started tossing the baseball around with a teammate while my mind wandered briefly wandered back to my family. My dad never missed a game once his career ended. My mom, on the other hand, missed some here and there due to her photography jobs. She accepted work when my dad forced her to. He told me he could see it in her eyes when she wanted to cover a story and that we needed to encourage her to go.

More than once, Dad and I had sat on the couch together and informed her that the house wouldn't burn down, I wouldn't flunk out of school, Jacey would have her lunch packed and homework done, and we'd eat three meals a day if she left us for a week. We basically had to convince the woman that we would survive in her absence.

Compared to other moms, mine was rare. More often than not, my friends' moms couldn't wait to leave the house and not be held accountable for what happened there while they were away. My family, on the other hand, practically shoved my mom out the door every single time. She never wanted to leave us. And to be honest, my dad wasn't the same when she was gone. He always seemed a little sad, no matter how happy he was with me and my sister.

When both games finally ended, the group of us always gathered at either our house or my uncle's for dinner; tonight it was our turn. Whenever we'd get together, Gran would rave about how much she loved being surrounded by family, but sometimes I wanted to kill my little cousins. Tonight Uncle Dean's nine-year-old twins were running around like they were possessed by demons, wanting to put makeup on me and paint my nails.

What was it with chicks? Why did they always want to mess with your nails? My sister encouraged their behavior, even after I warned her I'd throw her in the pool with her clothes on.

"You wouldn't!" She narrowed her green eyes at me.

"I would. And I will. Try me," I dared her.

"Enough," Mom chided from the kitchen. "Come in and eat. Girls, leave Chance alone. He doesn't want his nails painted today, but I bet your dad does." She smiled at Uncle Dean, and Aunt Melissa burst out laughing.

My dad walked over to my mom and planted an embarrassing kiss on her lips before giving my sister and me a squeeze.

When dinner was ready, we all sat at the table as the conversation flowed and the noise grew so loud it could probably rival an Italian family gathering in New York. About halfway through the meal, Dad calmed the table down, asking for silence.

"I have some important news I want to share with you guys," he said, leveling his gaze with mine. "Especially with Chance."

Once everyone had piped down, Dad announced with a big grin, "Fullton State has had a scout at the last few home games. They like what they see with Chance."

The whole table erupted into cheers, while my heart beat rapidly in my chest. Fullton State was the only place I wanted to play ball. I might not be a pitcher like my father, but going to the same college where he had started his career, and where he and my mom had met? To say it was my number one choice would be the understatement of the year.

"One of the coaches is retiring soon, which means they're looking for a new coach. So, if things work out all around, looks like you'll have to deal with me for another four years, Chance," he continued, winking at me.

"I wouldn't have it any other way, Dad." I shrugged, elated that my father would be there to continue molding me until I was ready for the major leagues. Some kids might resent their father micromanaging their sports participation, but I knew I was lucky. There was no one better than my dad when it came to baseball.

"Yeah, just stay away from all the, uh ..." Uncle Dean paused, glancing around the table at all the young girls before continuing. "... distractions out there. Make sure you get a background check on every slut who tries to seduce you."

"Dean!" Gran shouted from across the table.

"Oh my God! Don't listen to him." Aunt Melissa smacked his arm. "I mean, listen to him, but ..." She grunted and stopped short of finishing her sentence.

Uncle Dean smirked. "I'm just trying to warn him. Someone needs to."

Mom came around the table and patted me on the back. "Chance has his head on straight. He isn't a Little Jack. Don't you worry, he's focused. He'll be fine."

"I hope I get to go to Fullton State too," Coby interjected and my mom audibly sighed.

"I'm not sure I could live through history repeating itself," her widened eyes met my Aunt's.

"Two generations of Carter boys? Lord help us all," Aunt Melissa shook her head.

Before I could say anything, Dad scooted his chair back and pulled on my mom's hand, causing her to fall straight into his lap.

"I don't think using me as a bad example is really working here, folks." My dad frowned at the rest of the family while wrapping his arms around my mom's waist. "'Don't be like Jack,'" he said in a mocking falsetto voice. "'Focus. Don't be like your father.' But as far as I see it, being like me will get you the best wife in the world, the coolest kids, and a great family. Yeah, son …" He glanced at me. "Don't be like me. Wouldn't want that."

My mother practically melted as she gave him another less-than-appropriate kiss, no matter how many times I groaned. I watched, shaking my head, as my dad pulled two quarters from his pocket and tucked them into her hand. "For later," he whispered, but I heard and he knew it.

Damn it, Dad. I was ruined forever. But I wouldn't have it any other way.

I eventually wanted what my parents had … just not anytime soon.

Later.

WAY later.

Thank You's

First and foremost I have to thank every single one of my readers for their love, support, enthusiasm and encouragement. You all fell in love with Jack F'n Carter and his cast of misfits and I couldn't be more thankful or more grateful. The passion you have for these characters has overwhelmed me and frankly, you all make my day with your super hot pictures and quotes, casting boards, gifts, paintings, tweets, emails, etc! Thank you so much for your support. The success of this series is because of you- you made this book happen. YOU made this story come to life. THANK YOU. Always. I am eternally grateful for your bad-assness. <3

My family who is forced to support me even as I press ignore on my cell phone (sorry Momster and Brother Jim), or do my best to tune them out while I'm writing. Thank you to Blake and Point for seeing past my moodiness (aka bitchiness) and loving me anyway.

Throughout the last two years a team has formed in my professional life … a team that I couldn't live without when it comes to publishing my books. Thank you so much for your beautiful designs and creative energy, Michelle of IndieBookCovers. You are brilliant and patient and you always know exactly what I want. Love your talent. Thank you Pam

Berehulke of Bulletproof Editing for being with me since the very beginning. We're one bad ass team and I flip out at the mere thought of ever having to use another editor. Don't ever leave me. Lol :)

I think in the olden days (ha ha ha) a writer's journey was often a solitary one filled with days on end of loneliness and the longing that someone, ANYONE, would understand what the experience felt like. I'm so flipping blessed to be surrounded by not only some of the most talented ladies in the business, but those of which I consider friends. They have made this experience anything but lonely and my life is that much fuller because they're a part of it: Samantha Towle, Tara Sivec, Jillian Dodd, Kyla Linde, Shannon Stephens, Rebecca Donovan, Claire Contreras, Michelle Warren, and Tiffany King- thank you ladies for always being there when I need you.

There are others, who through this incredible age of the internet world, have been brought into my life. I'm so thankful that we have had the ability to interact, meet eachother and become true friends. To everyone I love new and old, thank you for your support in this journey. I appreciate you all so much: Catjacks, Becks, Christina Collie (feedback extraordinaire), Dani Van Z & Penny Mum, Melissa Mosloski, Jenny Aspinall & Gitte (Totally Booked Blog as well), Emily Lalone, Kristie W., Sali, all the girls in The Perfect Game Changer Group, and the real Jack F'n Carter (he knows who he is). I am so blessed.

About the Author

Jenn Sterling is a Southern California native who loves writing stories from the heart. Every story she tells has pieces of her truth in it, as well as her life experience. She has her bachelor's degree in Radio/TV/Film and has worked in the entertainment industry the majority of her life.

**Jenn loves hearing from her readers
and can be found online at:**

Blog & Website – http://www.j-sterling.com
Twitter – http://www.twitter.com/RealJSterling
Facebook – http://www.facebook.com/TheRealJSterling

**If you enjoyed this book, please consider writing a spoiler-free review on the site from which you purchased it. And thank you so much for helping me spread the word about my books and for allowing me to continue telling the stories I love to tell. I appreciate you. **

Other Books by This Author:

Chance Encounters

In Dreams

The Perfect Game - Book One

The Game Changer - Book Two

Thank you for purchasing this book.

Please join my Mailing List to get Updates on New and Upcoming Releases, Deals, Bonus Content, Personal Appearances, and Other Fun News! :)

http://tinyurl.com/ku7grpb